Remote control planet

Chapter one the end of Mars

One day in 30000 years, there was a major crisis in the MAS regime led by Stan. Stan was trying his best to solve this problem.

Stan was sitting in his chair, frowning, trying to deal with this planetary crisis.

Mars is on the edge of the Milky way. It is in a moderate position in the mulberry system.Originally, due to the rapid progress of civilization, horse star is in a booming development stage. As a result, in a galaxy trade, horse star's trade merchant king Huo happened to meet the son of a ruling class on Moore star because of selling fake goods. Under the guidance of experts, he learned that the prince of Moore star was angry and started a war with horse star.

In the vast galaxy, there are not a few planets with life, and each of them is unique, including their unique regime.

The social development stage of moor star is still in the feudal system, but the relationship between monarch and minister is harmonious, education is developed, and leaders of each generation have strong strength. Such family rule has lasted for a long time, but under the circumstances of population expansion and interstellar exploration, there are many different lineages.

Such is the example of a grumpy prince.

More or less, the current leader of moor has the military power of the planet.The deceived Prince is favored because he has his own army. Although it is not big, it is also small.

The main reason is that the power of Moore star is immeasurable. This army, Prince Moore, is not afraid to be completely destroyed.

Because their planet has the capacity of mass-produced biological people, who are not slaves, but the most loyal guards.

Highly unified spirit, weak self thinking, medium learning ability, but superior to its outstanding human sea tactics.

No one can fight without fear of death.

Stan went through the galaxy map and found that Moore star is also in the position of the Milky way, which happens to be an axisymmetric position with the Mars star Stan is in.

When he turned out another galaxy guide, Stan scratched his head again, because when he saw the introduction of the Moorish people, he found that they were really different. If the battle started, it was not certain who would win or who would lose.

Stan made a glass of whiskey, raised his legs and breathed slowly. He was thinking about whether the description on the data was accurate.

Because in the feudal society, the people of moorstar kept the habit of opening up territory, and the level of science and technology was several levels higher than that of the people of marshstar.

Because of their wild nature, the Moorish people often show such a domineering character in business.This has led to the fact that most of the deals between multiple life planets and the moors ended with less profit for merchants.Molesians are also very good at business, which normally leads to a trade deficit.

As a matter of fact, when things are out of sight, it's only right for you to recognize your achievements. This is the way of ordinary businessmen.Unfortunately, this time, the Mars man hit the muzzle of the gun.

Prince Moore is called Moore. Being favored proves that he is not only smart, but also has a strong wrist. He is a tough character.

The parliament of Mars is still discussing the details of the amendment to the trade law. Some members of parliament even proposed to amend the trade law of Mars, but these are not the issues Stan wants to think about.The military issue still needs the supreme leader to make a decision, in short, to wipe the bottom of the cheater businessman.

Merchant Huo Wang has entered the trial process, and the judge is ready to kill the star sinner.

Stan's office, watching the death broadcast, felt a burst of sadness and powerlessness.

□□"Almost!"Stan is almost crazy. He thinks the technology blockade has not been broken.

It's a mysterious eleven dimensional space. Before the death of the national master, he said that the energy is large, but the energy of Mars is not enough.

MASTAR then took a new path to promote peace and nature. Although they didn't invent the airship of light and couldn't make wormholes, they founded the Galactic trade center

Mars took the road of business, and naturally made a lot of money, but there were still people who were greedy for profits and became scum, such as the star war criminals who were unlucky to die today.

The mother planet can't be destroyed, can the desolate planet? There's not enough energy, can we sacrifice other resources in the universe to complete Mars?Maybe, but he can't wait for the army to arrive.

He opened the screen of the chief scientist, and there was a wise man dressing.

□□"I think if we want to kill the army from the perspective of eleven dimensional space, we need to change the entropy state in a directional way. In a simple three-dimensional way, we need to transform the kinetic energy into potential energy, and then into kinetic energy to kill them, but..." the self proclaimed scientist's tone is a little uncertain.

□□"If you can't lock it, you can't."

□□"What does that mean?"Stan asked.

□□"In a word, adults, even if you can't understand what I just said, you have to understand clearly that there is still a gap between our technology and theirs."The chief scientist sighed and shrugged helplessly."Soldiers to block, water to cover."

Stan clenched his fist and slapped the table hard.

□□"Issue a first-class warning order to the world, concentrate energy and meet the war!"

Chapter II the army's pressure on the border

　　Gold and iron horse, like a tiger.

At this time, the moor Empire seemed to eat the merchant family on the opposite side.

Stan fought north and south. I don't know if it was for other reasons. Seeing the Starfleet this time, everyone hid.

□□"Huh?Crawler? "Moore over there, seeing all the people hiding, with his political sense of smell, is obviously wrong.

□□"All the people are hiding. It may be a trick."Moore saw their reaction so fast that he felt something was wrong.

The black city will crush the Cloud City, and Jiaguang Jinling will open to the sun.

Two old foxes are waiting for each other to start.

□□"How do they understand space theory?"Moore didn't feel quite right, because along the way, he had been studying history books and the crossing of the galaxy, which had reached an unpredictable level.

　　"Eleven dimensional space can be overturned.We are here to express our heartfelt congratulations on behalf of the Moorish empire!Submit to me, submit to the family! "Moore opened the electromagnetic wave and shouted at Mars.

　　"Stan over there, who was already shaking, put the hiding place on his head and controlled the energy strike."

Only Moore looked up and saw the dark abyss.

Stan started PlanB with a shake of his hand.

Blue planet concentration station, it's a very powerful planet.All the preparations for life are in motion.

At this time, the first mock exam of the Star Wars war King Huo Wang, the mouth corners slightly, and roars loudly, then the hand goes to the bag, a crystal block of energy is pulled out by him.

The executioner standing in front of him was also slightly stunned. The last scene in front of him was a thick fire.

The distance between the execution platform and the battlefield is no more than 100 meters.

Seeing the fire, Moore's attention was once again attracted and slowed down.

However, the fire, accelerated to extremely fast, suddenly disappeared in space.

The next moment was next to Stan, who didn't even notice.

　　"Cowards know how to run!"Moore got angry and planned to take advantage of the victory.At the touch of a button, the anti particle system of the spaceship started slowly. Unfortunately, this look up, a look at the execution ground, and the time for acceleration made him stay for a long time.

Stan sacrificed all his expendables and moved the battlefield to earth.

It's just that Stan controls that button, and the backlash of his energy opens up the abyss.

Mars, to be destroyed, and his subjects, to be destroyed.

Stan is a dangerous chess player. His body crossing the void is very strong, but it doesn't mean that there is no protection measures.

After discussing with the chief scientist of Mars and the team of scientists led by him, we have come up with a plan: to move the battlefield while protecting ourselves.

This is based on the analysis of Moore's character, Stan made a great personal decision.

As long as Moore is attracted, destroying the planet is not his ultimate goal.He just wanted to vent his anger.

Stan didn't want to start a war, he was just a fighter. As the actual commander of the army, he had to do this. A planet, and ultimately to preserve the ethnic group, what he did was worth it, including sacrificing himself.

Stan speeded up to an amazing speed in a short time.And the death squads have provided him with enough energy.

But at this time, his energy is too strong, and the protection measures are not stable enough. At this time, he can't control it.The tearing sense of the body, together with the strong vibration and the violent friction out of the atmosphere, almost made him "dead".

Moore was angry at last, and his spacecraft began to show a strange situation: a flash of movement scared other Mars people who had not been affected by the radiation. The "eye of space" over Mars was broadcasting the battle live. Few people in the world who had not slept were staring at the screen to see the war.

Stan at the moment is a God and a devil in the eyes of the maassians.

Mars will soon die out.They don't know whether it's the end of the day or whether it's saving the people who don't know the truth. They have to turn off the TV and go back to sleep in the cave.

But it can be seen from the eyes that the radiation has spread slowly, which is irreversible.

□□......

At this time, the two men on the battlefield are actually competing tactics. Stan is taking the risk-taking route. His ability is not enough, so he is well prepared, including the protection armor planned by the previous team of scientists.

Moore is more elegant in fighting because he takes the lead in science and technology, but he has less flexibility than stan in fighting alone.

However, Moore can't give up. After all, if he wins this time, he will go back to his family. In addition to his fighting achievements in killing "lower creatures" and his latest understanding of space, according to the imperial system, 90% of the next king is him.Therefore, no matter how high the cost is, we should take this breath.

As for Mars, he doesn't care. It's just a living planet.

Stan seems to be at a shrinking point, so he goes backward to the particle accelerator. The faster he annihilates, the faster he finds that there is still a particle beside him, but he can't speak at this time.The physical body is almost completely emptied and belongs to the universe.

Naturally he knew who did it, but it was too fast to stop.Stan's goal is clear: a planet that's a little bit blue and a little bit alive.

Finally, it's time.

The body was all torn, Stan first became angry, and then suddenly disappeared inexplicably.

□□"It seems that the eleven dimensions can't be looked down on, I can't see..." Stan's fleet began to leap at full speed, but it will take a long time to reach Stan's speed.

Because its quality is too great.

Moore's eyes were fixed, and he looked at the body that had hit the grave, and he wanted to use it.

□□"In any case, it's all dead, and the country doesn't have to go back..." these powerful people, including deputies, can't resist the erosion of time.

□□"The twilight of the gods!"With Moore's eyes open, the whole man also burns the fleet together, turning it into dust.

Two waves of auroras hit Bermuda and Himalayas respectively.

For a moment, both of them were silent and there was no longer any fluctuation.

It's just that this revolution is happening quietly.

The blue planet, in a flash, got two huge impact forces, two shocks, even a small section of land covered by sea water.

It was a planet that had not yet given birth to life. Undoubtedly, the battle between Stan and Moore made it a little bit more alive.

Stan, Moore, including the Horowitz holding the energy block, entered the eleven dimensional space.

In the high dimension, this is rebirth and a new beginning

Chapter three the age of reptiles, evolution

I don't know how long it took. When the clouds and fog around these two places were scattered, there was a magical scene: sparks haunted the void, vaguely like a dragon circling, on the other side was obliterated by the ash hit by a huge mass of planets, and the continent sank.

From the point of view of the blue planet, this sudden change would have to wait a long time, because the external two man meteorite like fall changed the ancient ecosystem.

But how long can this campaign last?

Stan is still alive, but in a strange way, his bones are broken all over his body, there is a breath left, and his head is becoming more and more unconscious.

Beside him, there was a broken head and his unyielding eyes.That's King Huo, a war criminal who fought hard.

There are no protection measures. Unfortunately, otherwise, on the blue planet, with the resources and capabilities of King Huo, there is still a trace of vitality.

That energy block may be his last resource

Moore should be able to support them, both of them have their own dependence.

Fortunately, Stan only sacrificed a small team after decelerating. This Death Squadron is the most elite force of Mars, but it's Mars that makes him sad.

Mars will soon become a wasteland. The nuclear power's recoil force has destroyed 30% of the land, and it is still spreading. Moore also fell on the ground because of his pursuit of Stan.

Moore looked up and wanted to see the man farthest away. Unfortunately, there was no chance, only the faint debris and meteor sparks.

Can only fall asleep.

At the peak of Himalayas, Stan pinched his hands, mixed up the four substances, and then rolled them into a chain like spiral structure, one end at a time. Unfortunately, it's just a little bit short.

He took a look at the chain and hesitated, but it was too late to do it again.

So the whole man turned himself and the rest of Huo Wang into a flame and threw himself into the double helix deconstruction.

This is the stop codon.

The double helix structure, one end at a time, with the melting iceberg, turns into water and leaves slowly. The legend of Mars is still being copied.

Mars is not destroyed. It's just about to start over.

This is Stan's last chance to inherit for Mars.

□□......

□□"We still haven't succeeded, moles!"Moore sighed that he could not get up at all because of the earth's gravity, and his life was not long.

So Moore's hand delimited the void, and a blue and a green plant appeared.

A forward spiral, a reverse spiral.

One looks up to the sky and the other to the ground.

It's a plant, it's just in the water, it's going to be rushed to the deep blue sea.

Moore's head was askew, his stiff body lying on the ground.

He will also be dealt with naturally, dust to dust, earth to earth.

I seem to hear heaven singing.

□□"Alas, how dangerous it is!"

□□"It's hard to get to the green sky on the Sichuan Road!"

The hurricane is in Xijuan, but the dark clouds have dissipated. It's hard to see a bright sky.

No, it's not time.

Stan and Moore, in a sense, made the same choice.

　　"Go with the flow."

　　……

When MAS had the self-consciousness again, he found many of himself.

This is a very mysterious thing. I don't even know how long this time has passed.

　　"Big dream thousands of autumn, what year is tonight?"

　　"Change the name to Thomas."Stan smiled, and now he is himself.

What kind of body are you? At the moment of approaching the speed of light, you really don't understand what you are.

He woke up suddenly and looked at the world carefully again.He could not see the trace he planted.

One flower one world, one leaf one Bodhi.

He was the first to wake up, but not the last.Weird creatures with four legs, as Moore said, are really like reptiles.

He couldn't wait for him to get hurt. He saw a huge figure.

He vaguely remembers when it happened.

　　"Run!"He rocked his legs wildly, and the whole man jumped up, but before he landed, he was caught.

　　"Moore!"Thomas was a little confused and regarded the pterosaur in the sky as his enemy.

Just this time, the whole ground trembled.

The fire appeared again, and the reptiles and the flying dragon in the sky fell at the same time.

Thomas is very unwilling, he just hope that his efforts are not in vain.

Life, origin, extinction

Chapter IV thinking collision

　　From the beginning of spring and autumn, a hundred schools of thought contend.

Zigong stood on the official road and looked at the famous man, a nine foot man, who looked taller than him even when sitting in a car.

He regretted that he had met him so late and that he had spent these short decades.

Although, my business is booming.

It's time to leave.

Willow branches fluttered gently, spring breeze gently blowing his cheek.The blurred face in the distance became more and more clear: it was a teacher, his face was a little white because of the long-term poor life, sitting on the car, it was hard to cover his body's fatigue.

Although thin, but straight back and amazing height, let his hard angular cheek appear less domineering, more weak.

　　"Is this the master?"Zigong said with a smile, "it's not like a scholar, but like a businessman who has gone through many vicissitudes. However, such a life of travel is really yearning for."

Before Confucius could speak, he asked, "I've heard that my husband has traveled around the world, and I don't know what he thinks about governing the country."

The master looked at Zigong and was puzzled. He traveled around the world, and there were many people blocking his car because he was not convinced. But there were few people who asked political opinions directly like this. But the master turned his head and looked at Zigong's slightly gorgeous clothes, and then he knew who the Taoist was.

　　"Weapons, food, and the trust of the people."

□□......
According to the Mohist organization, Mozi is polishing his weapons.
□□"Love, not attack, and be wise to ghosts and gods."
□□"Fragmentation is a great shame for China."
□□"In our Greater China, when we are separated for a long time, we will be united. When we are together for a long time, we will be separated."
□□"I wait for that day!"
With a jerk, Mozi pulled the tough steel out of the molten iron and into the cold water.
When the white Qi is steaming, the iron sword is more and more fresh in an instant.
□□"Hoo... When a sharp sword comes out of its sheath, something important will happen in the world. We are weak in our ability, and we should do our last effort!"With a twist of his head, he saw two figures, one big and one small, coming to him.
□□"I can't agree more with the idea of Mohism."The slightly bent figure said.
With a tacit smile, Mo Zhai carefully put the sword back into the scabbard and saluted the old man.
□□"With your help, we will not worry about carrying forward the idea of Mohist school."
□□"Love both, not attack!"
□□......
□□"The way can be said, not the way!"The old man sat on the back of the blue bull and sang.
The farmer who just got up and rushed to the field saw only one person, one blue cow, walking far away in the early morning fog.
The farmer rubbed his eyes. When he wanted to see clearly again, the fog was gone, but the man and the cow were gone.
□□"Am I dazzled..." the farmer scratched his head and turned to work again.
The old man on the back of the blue bull looked at the common people and felt nothing.
□□"No more honing the world of mortals, just asking for it all one's life."
□□"When the emperor hears about it, he will die in the evening."
□□......
□□"The clouds are getting denser and denser, and the phenomenon of life is so thick that 80% of the chance can come."
□□"The eye of space", empty, eerily issued a lot of voices to discuss opinions.
And the horse star behind them has already been devastated.
After that time, it was a devastating blow to Mars, but also a new one to Parliament and the public.
□□"Near another land, we have sent out the first wave of consciousness transmission, and sent the technology of the spire there. This time, unlike Stan's rush, we considered the impact of reducing gravity and the environment. The first consciousness transmission also found the pure blood system.That is to say, we can also wake up his memory through the eleven dimensional spatial positioning method. "Mr. Li said.
Mr. Wang smiled bitterly: "we have done enough, and the incubation of life has come to this step. It can be said that in the future, we can only survive."
□□"Don't worry."Senator Xie interrupted their discussion."Regardless of our cost, although the space eye has experienced the phenomenon of machine aging, but in the Mars ephemeris, it can last for about 10000 years, which is enough for us to do something."
□□"What to do?"A virtual ID has spoken.
There was a total silence.

Senator Xie's electric signal is a little disordered, which is obviously caused by her strong mood fluctuation.

□□"I think that in the extreme state of machine collapse, we can transmit data from time to time, and then change the genes on the planet directionally to guide their changes, or even accelerate their changes."

There was silence again, but it didn't take long for someone to take action.

□□"I don't agree!"It's the famous councillor Zhang.

□□"You are following Stan's example!""Congressman Zhang seemed a little angry," Moore star in the back, lost a legitimate prince, has been very angry.Before there is a time crisis, after the pursuit of soldiers, how to talk about the limit!It was Stan who killed us without any defense! "

□□"But we understand that life is immortal. At least on the level of electrical signal, we have done it, haven't we?Without Stan, we can still live? "Councillor Xie retorted.

□□"Are you still you?Please answer my question head-on. "Councillor Zhang countered.

□□"Come on, the Council is not for you. Come on, show your hands."Mr. Wang said helplessly.

□□"No, I have a perfect plan for that."Senator Xie pointed to the void, and a picture of stars slowly unfolded.

□□"This is my observer plan."

□□......

The king of Moores tore up his proposal for re-election. At this time, he was ferocious and almost crazy.

□□"I command this last army in the power of the king!"

□□"I, the moors, have abdicated and never ascended the throne!"

□□"The next king will be Duanmu, Prime Minister. Moorish needs you to take the helm!"

A stone stirs a thousand waves.No one expected that the current king would not publish the list of successors, but directly declare his abdication.

Today is destined to be a bloody night.

The former king, with a million conscripts and three million clones, vowed to step on Mars.

□□"I will not kill all, dominate the universe, I moor star, where is the glory?"

□□"Son, I lost my throne for you."

□□"How about losing you and winning the world?"

Chapter V observer plan

When the former king of Moores marched into Mars with resources and hands, this group of data that lingered on the "eye of space" were trying to speed up the incubation of creatures on the blue planet.

A huge star map is displayed, showing two stars, one red and one basket. In the vast Star River, the two stars are insignificant, but they are in an axisymmetric position, with some special aesthetic feeling.

□□"According to the interstellar jump rules calculated by the team of scientists, information is transmitted from here to there. According to Mars, time has always been calculated, that is, not long ago."

□□"When King Moore hears about the loss of his beloved son, he will surely come in person and make a lot of preparations.With the technology of human cloning, we need to build a complete fleet.He also needs to spend a lot of energy and time on resource integration. "

□□"Moores are strong, but not the strongest, so they can jump only three times, and then they can only move at one percent of the speed of light."

Senator Xie pointed to the star map. It was a desolate planet.

□□"That's where 1288 is. It's still some distance from Mars. It's estimated that in the half-life of the space eye spacecraft aging, they will reach the parent star, that is, the time of the Mars calendar of 5000 years or so, by counting the time of refueling midway, the time of acceleration jump, and the time of one percent of the speed of light."

□□"If the accelerated incubation is successful, we can hide in the blue planet. With the data of the next generation, we can take the blue planet as the site to fight back. King Moore, who does not find his enemy easily, will not kill himself."

□□"If we don't hatch successfully, we can only enter the transmission station, dissipating the spacecraft energy to transmit us to the blue planet at one time. Someone will surely die in the middle, but the purpose of hiding can also be achieved."

"What we want is not just to linger, we want them to understand what is the power of Mars," said Senator Xie with a smile.If we don't fight again, we won't be able to recover the glory of the past. "

As soon as this is said, we all miss the former Galaxy Trade Center. The founder of the first generation is the man of Mars, who also created a lot of different atmosphere for the galaxy.According to the market regulations, if there is no horse race after ten thousand years, it will be regarded as giving up the market and being auctioned by auction houses to take over other life planets.

This is a fat poor, slightly pale horse star in the level of war. They can stand tall in business.

Making a fortune with a dull voice is the business model advocated by Mars.

Unfortunately, it's also commerce, destroying the planet.

They only hope that the vagrant will not come back and be disappointed when they see the red covered planet.

As soon as Senator Xie's words came out, they all resonated.

□□"I agree that we need to change our strategy and work steadily step by step."

□□"I don't agree. It's a disguised abandonment of our parent star."

After the fierce competition, Senator Xie's proposal received 55% support.

This kind of proposal with low support rate was supposed to be voided directly, but in a special period, there is another process, which is to submit it to the court and the Senate for joint decision.

The future of Mars can't be sloppy

□□......

At this time, on the blue planet, a great man slowly came to the throne.

Dressed in gorgeous clothes and a hat, he walked to the highest place gracefully.

At this time, thunder and lightning, wind and rain are coming.

Under the Afang palace, I don't know how much flesh and blood there are, surrounded by ghosts.

But this man will be remembered forever.

He seemed to be surrounded by thunder and lightning. When he went to the highest place, all the civil and military officials lowered their bodies to worship the emperor.

As he stepped inside the door, a gust of wind came violently.

It's raining.

In the palace surrounded by thunder and lightning, he roared to the sky.

□□"Unify the Jianghu for generations!"

□□"Crack."Lightning flashed through the void, illuminating his pale face, how great a man's power is.

His pale face, reflected by the electric light, is more frightening, more frightening, that is, his more wanton laughter!

□□"Hahaha!Hahaha! "

All the civil and military officials lowered their bodies and dared not look at this crazy man again.In the eyes of these people, some see fanaticism, some see cunning.

But don't worry. Who made him the first emperor?

Who else can ascend the throne besides him?Who else can hold the throne?

□□......

In the tavern, Jiang Ke is having fun in the tavern where Gao's singer is staying, ignoring Prince Dan's request.

When he was drunk, he fell asleep. Prince Dan would spit out old blood when he came back to this news through a spy.

Who let him so indulge in material desires, vertical and horizontal in the voice of dogs and horses? And the world said, he is hiding.Wise assassins are hiding themselves. They kill people with their swords when they are most happy and indulgent!

But in fact, he was afraid.

How can one capture King Qin alive?

So he put down his words and waited for a man.At that time, a noble man was the only one who appreciated him when he traveled around the world.

Of course, it doesn't include gradual separation.Gao Mingru, like gainie, could not see the strength of Jiang Ke at the moment.

After all, the Tao is different and we don't plan for each other.

Sometimes drunk, he often thought of his own ambitions.He repaired a letter and sent it away for a long time. I don't know when to return.

He didn't even receive a reply. How can he say that his wish can come true.

□□"Don't you even pay attention to me?Or deep in the chaos, involuntarily? "

□□"If you don't come, I'll go."That day, in front of Prince Dan, he saw Qin Wuyang's thin figure, murderous spirit around him, but it was just vanity.

outwardly strong but inwardly weak.

He was ready to retreat, but there was a thunder in the air, which surprised him.

Is this God urging me to leave?

□□"The wind is rustling and the water is cold. Once you go, you will never return!"

In the cold wind, I saw only a lonely figure, walking to the distance.

Gradually looked away, hands involuntarily snapped one.

String, broken.

□□......

Plan one has been implemented.

□□"Try to make this fight as long as possible. We need to slow down their technological evolution so as to hide ourselves when they run away."

□□"Did Stan go down this mountain in those days?"

□□"90 percent of the time, it's quite possible that this thriving culture doesn't seem to be as fast as they can get.There are also mountains on the left bank, which are just deflected by our first wave of transmission technology. The current evolution speed is still controllable. "

□□"We are still too compassionate. We give them these things. After all, they are all people who have no self-consciousness. Even if they deviate, they will grow into strong trees."

There was some impatience on the screen and said, "no, just destroy!Our plan is to slow down the process and take our technology as a guide when it comes!Only in this way can we have a dominant position. Remember, that's our escape base. We must grasp the first opportunity! "

The operator's back was cold, and he felt it was not a joke.

□□"Try to finish the task!"

Chapter six goodbye after thousands of years

Jiang Ke walked into the palace with dignity, holding a box and a map.

There was the general's head with a little satisfied expression. The general committed suicide for the great cause.His head became the ticket for Jiang Ke to enter the Qin palace

When he and Qin Wuyang stepped into the palace, they all felt the tension of the atmosphere.

It's depressing. It's depressing.Qin Wuyang never saw such a scene. He saw the majestic man in the palace, his body trembling slightly.

Jiang Ke, however, held the picture with his head down and dared not look up.As an assassin, keeping calm in front of the enemy is the top priority.

A little forward, a little further forward.

His head was already sweating slightly, and the king of Qin was very close. Within five steps, the head must be harvested in his hands.

It's just this task. It's changed to live capture.

He slowly unfolded the scroll, and looked closer and closer to the end. The hidden short blade would soon appear.

Qin Wuyang suddenly shakes and the first emperor picks his eyebrows, as if he is aware of something.

□□"Wait!"The first emperor ordered.

□□"I haven't seen the king in front of the hall. I'm very nervous. Please forgive me."Jiang Ke made a salute, then suddenly pulled the map, and finally the scroll reached the bottom.

The picture shows the poor dagger.

At this time, Jiang Ke's quiet and clear eyes looked at the first emperor in the palace.The knife in his hand suddenly loosened.

This is the first time that he faced the first emperor completely and straightly, saw his appearance, and flashed a trace of confusion and doubt.

□□"I'm familiar with him. Is he... Moore?"

This thought flashed in Jiang Ke's mind.

It's too slow. The time has passed.

This assassination turned into a chase war.

□□......

□□"Plan one failed!"

The commander was a little nervous, and the man behind the screen stopped shouting.

The commander knows that this is his last command career.

The boss won't let him stay in the group safely.

☐☐"Carry out plan 2, commander 1, freeze consciousness for one earth year, and erase the group's memory!"

Commander one shivered.

I didn't expect such a heavy punishment this time.

He glanced at the task evaluation form: "this task, failure."

☐☐"Mission initial level, level B.After the re evaluation of the group, it was upgraded to S-level. "

☐☐"The judgment of commander one shall be executed immediately!"

☐☐"Second plan, continue to kill!And lock the eleven dimensional coordinates of Jiang Ke and confirm his identity! "

All the people of the observer's plan found the unique place of Jiang Ke.According to their calculation, there must be some unusual reasons for the assassin to make mistakes at such a critical moment.

They firmly believe that Stan, who has passed on from generation to generation, has and only has a real body, hidden in these people.

But now we need to spread the Internet to save this great hero.

☐☐......

A few days later.

In the tavern melancholy gradually leaves, still plays the piano and drums for the guests, but has no previous atmosphere at all.

When he heard the news of Jiang Ke's death, he still felt as if he had passed away.

There is no emotion to caress the strings. The strings have been broken several times these days.

Even the best drum beating has lost its rhythm due to frequent wandering.

This is his last performance.

☐☐"The wind is bleak, the water is cold, and the heroes are gone forever..." the rhythm and melody, as well as the gradually departing aria, seem to be less exciting than before.

Gradually away from know, singing this song, he will be exposed to the public.

Boya and Ziqi are different.

When he put away his harps and ready to leave.

A man caught him.The stranger said with a smile, "I don't know if it's Jianli brother?"

Gradually away from the heart of a Deng jump, only that the event is not good.

☐☐"Want revenge?"Said the man.

Gradually away to hear this sentence, the guard suddenly took off half.No matter who he is, it's just his own.

They walked into the tavern and talked for a long time. When they left, they were more determined.

The strange man saw that he was leaving gradually, his mouth was slightly raised, and then the whole man gradually became transparent, and finally dissipated in the air.

It's just a solid projection, and Mars has dissipated a lot of energy for this task.

Gradually away will be hidden, using all his life to kill King Qin.

Opportunity, only once.

I don't know that what he is going to face is the pain of losing his eyes.

Chapter VII tower Kingdom

Alex woke up to find that he had been assigned to the blue planet.

It's a punishment of the earth year, but this body is still so fresh.

Alex was a little confused, confused about the passage of time.

He was suddenly surprised to find that this was not the most important thing.

□□"Have our people mastered the technology of biological cloning?The so-called moor star fleet has a lot of power! "

As a member of the group, he can still remember these words.

This so-called erasing memory is just a poor hypnosis.

Alex covered his head with pain.

Enough is enough, can't continue to remember.

There is someone on the top of the head.

This is quite a journey, never to return.

All of a sudden, Alex realized that the truth of the matter was far from simple, and the other possibility he thought of made him tremble a little.

□□"Do not see Tathagata."

He chewed these words out of his mouth, and never dared to go on.

He felt a sense of unusual in his heart with a sharp tremor and deep fear.

It's on an alien planet. There's a killing machine.

□□"Earth, is that the name?"

Alex's eyes flashed a little confused, as if they were uncertain.

□□"Anyway, call it that first."

Born a noble, low-speed aircraft equipped, so that he can quickly reach any place in a few seconds.

□□"It's good to be a ruler!"

Alex smiled and stopped thinking about other things.

Let's just muddle along in this life of intoxication.

All of a sudden, he found that those so-called people standing in the eye of space at the peak looked superior to others, but in fact, they were just some clowns.

□□"I don't understand you, and I don't need to understand you."Alex smiled contemptuously, and with a wave of his hand he put the low-speed aircraft in his sleeve.

At his feet, overlooking is the masses, there are some slave owners are driving messengers suffering people.

Alex took a close look at the towering tower buildings over there.

Yellow appearance, soaring to the top of the cloud.

It is worthy of being the most precious wealth left by all scientists.

Whether it's in terms of reducing gravity, or in terms of its precision sand carving, this is the only advanced technology of Mars.

The main preparation for a beautiful self-defense counterattack, but this tower is filled with cold silicon-based life.

I'm waiting for your attachment.

Now that this step has been achieved, what does it matter if the so-called clone does not clone or empathize?

In fact, Alex also knows how a person's power can withstand the times.

When he was in danger, he felt like a hero.

Now he felt like a bear.

When the dog is happy, it can also trample on the ants, and enjoy the wealth.

Basically, he didn't get any technology from the eye of space.

A tramp, destined to become a shepherd, is just a lamb on his side, not to taste it.

"If they are not, they are all false."

He looked at the overflowing River, but he could not shake his heart, just like the long-term impact, and could not shake the powerful spire technology.

That's the joy of great force, though it doesn't belong to him.

He will build hundreds of towers and make this place as hard as steel.

We may be able to counterattack against extraterrestrial civilizations.

Tonight he looked up at the glittering eyes of space and fell into deep thought.

......

Losing sight gradually, the strength of beating the drum is greater.

Several years of time, let his mind more broad, firm.

His hearing, however, gradually declined because of his playing the piano, drums and harps all the year round.

However, only in the evening when the wind began to ring, he followed the wind and heard the howling sound of ghosts and wolves, which reflected the voice and smile of Jiang Ke in his mind.

He can't forget it, so whenever the parade team is coming, he will hold the drum and knock louder.

"Listen to the cheering drum, are you happy? I just want to kill you."

Nails into their own flesh and blood, and then pull out, blood slowly dripping on the drum skin, bright and charming.

It's just that he can't see it anymore.

He swung his hands hard and his drum Club gently.

He didn't hear the echo.

It's not that there must be echo if you keep thinking about it?

I can't forget that man.

I can't forget that feeling.

He went to the execution table and was ready to cut himself off.So I jumped to dust and dissipated in the world.

......

In the hall of Parliament, no one spoke again.

"Do you want to save him?"Senator Xie pointed to the location. "The mission has failed. We don't need to save it."

"But later, when he has gone through thousands of reincarnations, what is left?"Councillor Zhang was a little excited.

"He's not a hero. He ruined us."Thank you for laughing.

"Once upon a time, I thought our plan was perfect."Councillor Wang knocked on the table."Now you have exchanged attacks and defenses, opinions and mutual recognition?"

Mr. Xie was a little sad. He looked at Mr. Zhang and said bitterly: "before we arrived at this place, we were husband and wife.Now it's not. We're MPs. He's just a loser. I'm just a mad girl. "

"Don't bring personal feelings here!"Councillor Wang is in a row of tables.

"Plan to continue!It's a long way from half-life!We have to hold on! "Said the councillor Wang.

With a scornful smile, Senator Xie said coldly, "there are some data on the deck that have disappeared."

　　"I can't wait."

Chapter 8 battlefield, earth

　　The first emperor was safe and sound, but after his death, a very large scale of burial and the system he left behind were buried in the world.

Before his death, he issued a decree to the people beside him: no more contact with people outside the state of Qin.

At the first emperor of the hall, it's ridiculous to see that people have to take a detour.

Even if he had already closed the temple of Mount Tai, there was no such heat and blood.

As soon as the emperor died, there was a political struggle.

All kinds of characters are like clowns, with the appearance of pink ink.

The eye of space has coveted this for a long time.

But when the first emperor died, what was his soul?

It's either Moore or Stan, as most of the members speculate.

But they couldn't figure it out.

As for Jiang Ke, he had already died under the siege of the people.

How difficult it is to capture his electric signal.It's like after a particle collides, it will disappear in a second.

The space eye near Mars limits the ability to capture electrical signals.

Next time, when?

　　......

Alex is ready to enter the tombstone. The golden shell is ready for him.

The body came to an end, and all that remained was to fall into an endless sleep.

The pyramid of Hoover, a great architectural miracle that can surprise the world, is an architectural complex integrating attack and defense. Alex is the key to suppress this architectural center. People made gold armor for him to show their respect.

However, he was not in a good mood. He wanted to go back, but he had a bad feeling.

Sure enough, he received a message from far space.It's from the eye of space.

　　"Operator 0523, you've landed on earth in violation of the eye of space law, and now it's time to go back to the eye of space."

　　"However, the eye of space is facing the problem of energy exhaustion, which can't lead you back to the eye of space, so please find the next host on earth and prepare for the earth's counterattack."

　　"Our main battlefield will be the earth."

Doodle doodle

The signal is off.

Alex was upset for a while, but he had no way, no data traction, he could only stay on the earth.

The bodyguard came in and slowly covered him with a golden shell.

His eyes suddenly opened, and the bodyguard's eyes were full of data.

Then Alex's body was destroyed.

The bodyguard was a different person.

　　"Is that the feeling of immortality? It's a pity that you can't go back home."The guard sighed.

New Arrakis, reborn.

□□......

In the eye of space.

Mr. Xie, Mr. Wang, Mr. Zhang and others voted, and finally decided to use plan a of the observer plan to accelerate the incubation of planet life, transfer data into the blue planet for the final counterattack.

The rocket shaped head of the eye of space is slowly aiming at the blue star.

Goal, Rome, Greece, Europe.

Boom!

A brilliant blue light rushed to the earth, and countless data streams with countless lives rushed to these three places.

□□"Eye of space, fall!"

The huge spacecraft suddenly separated and disintegrated into countless pieces, which hit the earth's surface.

At the same time, at the other end of the Milky Way universe, the king of Moores is very close to earth.

Although this approach is only a general one.

□□"The third jump!The speed of light is close to five percent! "Captain.

□□"Son, if you are not dead, I must help you back."The king of Moores clenched his fist, and it was through this belief that he could keep up to this point.

At this time, the earth is full of vitality, especially in Asia. The flame of civilization began from the imperial system and broke out quietly.

Europe and Rome, Greece and China, these four places, the door of trade also quietly opened.

If we take the analogy of interstellar relations, China at this time is like the moor star, while Europe, Rome, Greece and other regions are the beginning of the trade tradition of Mars.

The two regimes, on this blue planet, have evolved again, as if they had come back from the dead and gained new life.

It is the territory of Egypt that is not in line with this area.

Egypt, originally full of vitality, should not have presented such a morbid color at all in that era.

That's the color of loess. The green color has long been attracted by the invisible power of the pyramid. It has turned into a golden yellow. The sky over Egypt is forming a half spherical matrix, and each matrix is maintained by the energy of the spire.

It's the class a war criminals, the controllers, also known as Alex who control all this.

They are bound to live and die with the earth.

Chapter IX outbreak of war

It's a deep night. It's not so quiet.

This is Alex's third generation. Fifty years later, he has changed three bodies.

He was at the top of his power, the level of Pharaoh.

But even in immortality, sometimes there are problems.

For example, memory disorder, a little can't remember who they are. When they are sleeping, they often recall the past. When they wake up, they are confused.

Today is a different day, although he is a little confused, he also broke his fingers and calculated it carefully.

Today is his fiftieth earth year as the actual ruler of Egypt.The congressman in the eye of space, after sending that signal, has not contacted him for 50 years.

He is not lonely. He has unique carbon based life here, and he is much happier to live with them than to perform tasks in the eye of space.

But tonight is also an unusual night.

Because over Egypt, the moon, a satellite monitored by the main pyramid, suddenly lost its color.

Tonight, Alex looks into the night sky, remembers the past, and often pays attention to the dynamics of the planet.

Although the technology he has mastered at present can integrate attack and defense and monitor the dynamics of the solar system in real time, he still has no foundation for some high technologies.

For example, the wormholes of interstellar transition produce enough energy to cover up the light of the moon.

Is it coming?

All of a sudden, the moon returned to light.

Everything seemed normal and nothing strange happened.

Alex was relieved. He was a little tired.Although it was a little strange just now, it was not in his eyes.

Just as he was undressing and ready to sleep, a strange man came into being.

It was in the direction of the moon that the white light turned blood red.

Alex looked at the moon, his mouth twitched, and thought, "is it necessary to make such a big formation?"

However, although he thought about it in his heart, he was merciless.

He pressed the button for the attack.

□□……

□□"Report to the captain that we have reached the planet 1289, with a civilization level of 2D, excellent ecological environment, suitable for breeding life..."

□□Data error, data error, updating data

□□"Most of the civilization of the planet is D, and one is a!"

The men on the spaceship were in a hurry, as excited as if they had found a new continent.

□□"1289 was originally a recognized dead star, but a battle accelerated its evolution. I'm right, captain."The king of Moores squinted his eyes and said.

□□"Yes, but now, there's a big problem."The captain sighed, then picked up the microphone and shouted to the whole crew, "all units, please pay attention, all units, please be ready for defense immediately!"

The king of moor star snorted, "it's not enough to be afraid. When did I ever fear this, a small class a civilization, a warship of moor star's class s civilization.Defend with all your strength and be ready to fight back! "

□□"Yes!"

□□……

Now, the earth, planet 1289.

A violent wave of energy makes the magnetic field around a little disordered. The crushed stones are lying in the ground, as if they are shaking gently.

From the bottom four corners of the pyramid, four mechanical arms are extended, and then the four mechanical arms will be together to form a pyramid shape.At the top of the pyramid, there is a dark blue light, gathering energy and slowly delivering it to the tip of the four mechanical arms. Hundreds of pyramids are doing the same thing.

All the robotic arms have their own tilt angles. Obviously, the right place to aim is the moon, the blood red moon. That's where the battleship of the king of Moores stays.

Alex launches the order to remove the shield.

Alex launches the command, the energy gathers.

Alex, launch the command, launch!

A flash of a laser beam, not as big as you can imagine, but a small laser beam with a diameter of only three meters.

It hit the ship's shield exactly.

To be more precise, it broke through the protective cover of the spacecraft.

Straight through the ship.

And directly through the head of the king of Moores.

All the people on the deck were shocked.

Is that over?

Suddenly someone shouted, "that's the disintegrated cannon!"

Everyone panicked.

Decomposition gun, the product of SS civilization.

They forget that only the class a civilization of Mars started with trade.

It's not hard to get the cannons on the black market.

Its only function is to decompose all the media that can be decomposed.

Soon, the ship will disintegrate. Without the ship, everyone on board will be in a dilemma: no air. Without air, we can only wait for our own death.

It's ridiculous. Success is trade, failure is trade.

Only the captain was very calm, he looked at the body of the king of moor star, neither sad nor happy, but silently pressed the counterattack button.

For the last time, the ship made a lamentable roar, and then separated and disintegrated.

Alex saw that the color of yin and red on the moon faded away, and the corners of his mouth rose slightly, showing the smile of victory.

However, at the next moment.

Alex's pupils widened a lot because he saw something that frightened him.

□□"Antiparticle gun, God!"Alex groaned.

The last thing he saw was the back of his body, because his head had been separated from his body.

The powerful mechanical arm on the top of the pyramid disappeared because of the anti particle gun.

The pyramids are no longer the light of the past, and the civilization in this area is beginning to degenerate.

Everything is because of the short war.

Chapter 10 the age of talents

　　Tesla waited quietly for the result.

At 7:17 a.m. on June 30, 1908, a huge fireball crossed the sky with the same brightness as the sun.

A few minutes later, a strong light lit up the whole sky. Later, the shock wave generated by the explosion shattered the window glass within 650 km nearby.

The shape of mushroom cloud is quietly growing. On this day, the light from all over the sky sprinkled on the land of Siberia. Although Tesla had predicted for a long time, it did not know so accurate information.

He stood there quietly and exclaimed that heaven and earth did not take everything as a cud. The ice comet hit the earth and caused such a huge movement. He did not know how many people died.

Fortunately, the landing site is over Siberia, which is sparsely populated. The energy fluctuation is very large, but under his precise calculation, the surrounding villagers evacuated early.

There should be no casualties.

Thinking about it, he started the experiment of energy transition to protect the earth from destruction, energy can be transported, and even create more powerful weapons.

A tower, a coil, a weapon called "deadlight.".

□□……

He is a pharmacist without money.

His life is so poor that he can hardly support it.

But he still developed quantitative analysis, redox titration and other methods to analyze chemistry. Although he has never been looked at seriously in his life, after his death, he was awarded the title of analytical chemist.

He's Moore.

□□……

At that time, Einstein was young, but he got a strange disease, nothing, it was a minor disease.It's just that the hair on the head is a little "flowing". It can't be combed well.

There seems to be a huge amount of energy in every hair, because the heads connected by these hairs are not ordinary.

He studied the photoelectric effect and won the Nobel Prize. He also studied the theory of relativity. For example, in the micro world, the speed of light can not be exceeded.

He has made a great contribution to our humanity.

□□……

Hawking, or we can translate his name into "King Huo".

After all, he was in the same state as king Huo, who had wandered to the earth.

He has a rare disease, muscle atrophy, gradually lost the right to walk, speak.

But in this case, he has developed famous theories such as black hole radiation.

He often came back to dream that he was a war criminal and rushed to the earth with an energy block.

It was one of his nightmares.

Because his final result is not willing to die, his business has not been completely completed, it turned into a rotten corpse.

He had some hate and some relief.

Now, it's good.

□□……

In the age of talents, all four masters have left us.

Human beings have never lost their way in finding their own direction. We always believe that the source of human beings is like this.

However, a letter broke the situation.

People began to think about their origins, where they came from and where they should go.

First letter new student

Dear brother Lu:

I haven't seen you for a long time. I remember that I graduated from high school when I met last time. I'm really amazed that time is fleeting and time is fleeting.

Although I seldom surf the Internet, I also know that you are now an internationally renowned psychiatrist.I'm sorry to have trouble as a friend today.I heard that your undergraduate course is physics, so you won't be unable to understand what I'm talking about.You don't have to wonder. You can see it.

There have been many rumors among the people, saying that since the human history period, the great flood is a dividing line, and few historical data have been found forward.

We know that the great flood has excerpts in the ancient books of various religions. Let alone whether these religions have crossed regional restrictions and influenced each other, but we have reason to doubt that human beings have had a glorious civilization before, but it has been mercilessly erased by history.

Even in history, people like Muhammad and Jesus can only be recorded. That time was like being wiped out by a huge tractor, dragging his heavy mechanical arm.

You may wonder why I got involved in such a seemingly unrelated event, but it was a dream a few days ago that made me feel some incredible power.

The dream background is blank. As time goes on, a lot of words emerge on the white background gradually. I don't need to wait and see them clearly in my mind with the appearance of the handwriting. That text is still fresh in my memory until now:

□□"I am you. The Lord appointed you as the history inspector. Now the indigenous people on the earth you live in have restless thoughts. Their technology is slowly improving, but it will be exponential growth soon.Your task is to block the progress of human beings in this world. There is more than one history of monitoring. You don't know each other's identity, but you can detect them through their reactionary behavior.Don't believe in others, believe in yourself. Otherwise, the Lord will come down again, and this time there will be no hope of escape. "

This dream is very strange. The first one is that I still remember it vividly. The second one is that it has nothing to do with history.What is "I am you"?I have looked up religious classics, which is exactly the same as the concept of "reincarnation". It is also a concept mentioned in various religions (Dayu is a folk legend, and Nuwa mends the sky also has a record of releasing the flood. We will record them as religions for the time being).

The third is that after the dream was revealed, many images of different stages of civilization appeared in my mind. Although they flash by, they are very clear, which helps to confirm the possibility of reincarnation.

I don't know if it's the task of predicting dreams or inheriting my previous life. Naturally, I don't want the risk of destruction on the earth, so the first reaction I wake up is resistance. I've been wondering about many things, such as the self similarity in nature, such as the relationship between the left and right spiral rule in nature and biological form.Do these confirm the reality that we are remote controlled?

I've seen many doctors, especially in psychology and psychiatry.Some of them believe and some don't believe the view of previous life, because some doctors have come across some similar cases, and some doctors have come up with "dream analysis" to interpret such a phenomenon with me.

I haven't been diagnosed yet, but I've been crazy about reading and thinking these days.

The most amazing thing is not that, but since that night, I have had a lucid dream every night. I can't control myself in the dream. I can only follow the direction it guides me to move forward. Every time I have a chance to see the reflection surface, I will see the face that is not much different from my present face, which makes me more convinced of the existence of this matter.

These days of experience, let me have a great touch in both the outlook on life and values, I like to get a new life, but also have a deep sense of powerlessness: even if we dig out the secret, there is the so-called opportunity to resist?If something should come out, wouldn't it be inevitable?Anyway, I decided to take a chance with you.

Let me go back and comb again. First, I have a lucid and deep memory dream. My previous life has a task. My task is to prevent human development.Second: if the first point holds, then we are under control.Third, I have different dreams every night. Every dream is disordered. Next, I will screen out several scenes according to your reply suggestions and interpret some clues.

Once again, I would like to pay my high tribute to you. My friend, I hope you will reply soon. Maybe you can discover some different secrets in me.

□□   Your good friend: Zhang Lin.

First reply

　Dear zhang

I haven't seen you for a long time. I miss you very much. It's a kind of luck that we can reply to each other through Internet mail now.When can I see you?I'm curious about your experience.

Your last proposal is good. I think we can dig out your secret. What if all this is true?

In my long career as a psychiatrist, many people know their past lives through hypnosis.As for your situation, I really don't know.We call the consciousness which is beyond the subconscious of our body world as the superconsciousness, but because of the limitation of our body, we can't communicate with our superconsciousness.

In my cognition, the spirit is beyond the material, even if it is not, it promotes and restricts each other with the body.As soon as this conclusion comes out, you may have doubts: we have been taught materialism since childhood. Now how do you point to idealism?Are you a dualist?

I have to explain my opinion in detail first.First, material determines consciousness. I agree.But I believe that one of the statements is that the spirit depends on the material, and the spirit is expressed through the material.In Buddhism, there is a dispute between crossing people and crossing oneself, but which side thinks that the suffering of the body is a kind of test, a kind of cultivation, what is the test?It's the spirit, not the body, that tests. So that's what we mean when we say bad skin.

Secondly, as for your view on previous life, I have come across many such examples in my work, and I don't think I can explain this with just some theoretical things.Isn't it true that China has set a new technological record recently?Quantum entanglement may explain all this.Quantum entanglement means that after quantum entanglement, they behave the same and are not limited by time and space.This shows the connection between the superconsciousness and the body consciousness.

If you compare the superconsciousness to a function, then the space-time you are in is the set of corresponding solutions.If people can communicate with superconsciousness, it's equivalent to a U disk inserted into a computer. You can read the previous information, and the subsequent information can also be expected through this.

Einstein's theory of relativity has a scale effect, which indirectly proves the unity of time and space.Our superconsciousness is in my heart an imaginary "end of time."

It transcends our existing dimensions, incarnates in tens of millions, and makes his choice in various periods of time, so that whether it is in the past or in the future, it actually has a conclusion.So some people are able to see the previous life, which is likely to be the process of hypnosis to communicate with the superconsciousness.Now we have little research in this area, you may be a typical case.

Here I introduce a book "life is immortal", which has a great influence on me in my career.The past life may be certain, because in our dimension, time can only move forward and not backward, but I think there is still infinite possibility in the future.Why materialism science?Because we imagine such a scenario: if you want to choose bread and drink, you can only buy one. Your choice is not only your own choice, but also social influence. For example, your mother likes to eat bread, and you eat bread together with your mother when you were young, so you choose bread, while society and people are objective, and your decision must be based on material.

But imagine that last week you had a fitness card and if you didn't go, you would still choose bread.But if you go, the coach will tell you to eat less bread, which is high in calories.This shows that your choice is not only determined by the habit of a long time, but also by the influence of some recent people.In this way, a choice of variables will be very large, and will not evolve in a fixed direction.This is in contradiction with the conclusion I just said about the future.

Maybe it's my shortsightedness. Limited by this dimension, I don't know the past life, the future, the superconsciousness and whether the future is conclusive.But what I want to say is that the extended discussion is really interesting.

I'm not sure about your situation. Let's meet and make sure about your situation.Don't worry too much. Everything will be OK.

Your friend: Lu Minyue

Chapter 11 Duke Zhou's dream interpretation (1)

It's 3 p.m. in the cafe. It's quiet. It's not supposed to be photographed in this place. But a man lowered his cap and peeped under it.If you can see the eyes under his hat, you will show helplessness and fear, and sweat will flow all over his face.

The famous psychiatrist saw this scene, shook his head, put his hands together, and said to himself, "I really think I'm mentally ill. In the summer, I'm armed, and I'm not afraid to be seen and called the police."

Lu Min walked slowly into the cafe, wearing a pair of white gloves, a suit and a magic hat on his head. He looked very elegant and elegant. It's hard to imagine that he did such a job.

When the man in the cap saw the elegant gentleman, he quickly got up and smiled a long time ago. He hugged Lu Minyue, then took off his mask, took off his hat and said with a long breath, "I'm so hot."

"That's the first thing you said to me, boy!"Lu Min clapped the man on the shoulder, and they looked at each other and smiled.Although there was no one at this time, all the people present looked at the two of them.They also sat down very tacitly, looked at each other in the eye, did not speak to each other, and looked at each other carefully.

At that time, Lu Min broke the silence in time, and said, "that's a good saying. When a friend comes to you for help, he comes to borrow money from you.It's embarrassing for you to let me work overtime without borrowing money. "

□□ Did not expect such a joking words to make the atmosphere embarrassed, Zhang Lin said an inappropriate sentence: "the fate of all mankind is not counted."The smile on Lu Minyue's face suddenly stiffened. He was silent for a while and then said: "I don't know why you are like this. I remember that you used to like playing basketball, which is very lively.But now, because of a dream, it's like this? "

□□"Fart!"Zhang Lin's face turned red. "Do you understand what I'm talking about? Have you seen my dream? Do you know how helpless I am in my heart? Look, look!"He pointed hard at his clothes. "What is my dress up for? Now I'm banned by psychiatrists all over South China. They don't want to see me again. They say I have no medicine to cure."

Lu Minyue pressed his hand and made a silent gesture, saying, "if you change me, I'll see you come to the doctor again and again, preaching the end of the world every day, and I think you are a member of the cult.You see, your performance is not normal now. "

Zhang Lin calmed down, the red on his face gradually faded, and then became pale. The whole man fell on the chair like mud, closed his eyes, and several lines of clear tears flowed out of his eyes.

□□"It's not that I'm cold, it's that I've experienced so many things like this. You know, doctors in South China are very strong, but they are not as famous as me. Why?Because I can hypnotize, I know the dream. Duke Zhou's second is me, Lu Minyue.You can rest assured that I've met it, whether it's a psychological cue or a real experience.There is no materialism or idealism here.I just believe in what's in front of me. "The more calm Lu Min said.

□□"Well, you take me away. I'm going now."Zhang Lin is excited."Don't think about it. You're in a state where even if I'm a self-confident hypnotist, I can't cure you right away.We need your cooperation.Come on, give me your coffee. Stop drinking. Have a glass of white water. I'll let you get into shape later. "Lumin sipped his coffee gently, as if he had emptied himself.People who know him well know that when he's nervous, he'll take a sip of coffee, relax, and then listen with all his heart.

□□ Seeing him like this, Zhang Lin naturally relaxed and said casually, "let me tell you something about me.My dream is very strange, but there are many previous lives, among them are some more strange scenes, for example, I saw that I said a child into the fire, for example, I stood alone in the street helpless.These are clips that flashed back many times a night.And then there's the loop.I don't believe what's wrong with the cerebral cortex will disturb my mind, and I can't explain that feeling.In a word, I think according to your opinion, it may be that my general system is broken, sending me some chaotic information to accept, which is not interfered by time and space, so the end of the world may not be now, but it is very likely... "

□□"It is very likely that it will burst out at a critical point, and the introduction may be the rapid development of human science and technology."Lu Minyue answered."As like as two peas," I feel that now, exactly what you just said.The most frightening thing is the unknown. I have said a lot to you in my letter. One of them is the controlled unknown.If that's true, we may really have to do something. "

Lu Minyue shrugged and said, "five five year plan, I don't think it's likely to happen. Your analysis is very reasonable, because I've thought about many possibilities on the way to get together these days.What I said in my letter may be just an assumption. If you follow my reasoning, it's good to think of it here.Waiter, pay! "

Luminyue put down the cup in his hand, waved, took out his wallet from the bag of his coat, took out one hundred yuan and gave it to the waiter, then grinned: "this meal is for me. The medical fee is free.Well, it's good enough for you. "

□□"Don't be poor with me!"Zhang Lin looks decadent. His hands are placed casually, like a puppet held by someone: "what if human beings are really destroyed?"

□□ Lu Minyue straightened his clothes and said, "if you have the ability, don't behave like a real psycho all day long.Let's go. "

Chapter 12 Duke Zhou's dream interpretation (2)

They came to Zhang Lin's house. Lu Minyue hypnotized Zhang Lin.Although Lu Minyue was very relaxed at first, he could not help rubbing his hands in a strange environment.Looking at Zhang Lin's house, he saw that the color was actually the wall style with red and blue intersecting. He smiled two times and said, "yes, you've thought about this since graduation."

□□"That's color architecture!"Zhang Lin said, "I have a girlfriend. I'm not married yet.Red and blue can help me think deeply. Don't dawdle, hurry up. "

□□"Good!"Luminyue said, "you go to bed first, put yourself in a good mood, I will let you into the state."

□□"Don't you take this off?"Zhang Lin pointed awkwardly at Lu Minyue's gloves and hat."Come on, what do you know? My name is cosplay. It's a new hypnotic method.I don't look like a famous detective now. "Lu Minyue patted his clothes. "I don't spend money on enjoyment, I spend money on blade."

□□"But your hobby is strange.In the name of work, let your hobbies break out.Don't fix this. Don't you and I understand each other? "Zhang Lin lies on the bed, enjoying her face."I understand. I understand.Brother, put your hand out. "Said Lu Minyue.

□□"OK."Zhang Lin put out her hand and Lu Minyue took out a needle from the bag.

□□"I......"Zhang Lin almost broke his tongue, but Lu Minyue took back his hand holding the needle and said seriously: "work is my hobby, but I need your cooperation.Do you feel the pain at the tip of the needle?Wait, no matter what you see, don't be surprised. "

Zhang Lin's face was tired: "I've experienced what is called dream stealing space. You are here to steal my dream.But it's a pity that I'm your test object. There is no self awakening person in all.Let's not go through the process.Let's get started.You don't think I'm a quiet and beautiful man. In fact, my heart is quieter and calmer. "

□□"I can't speak with consumptive words, but I can still speak!"Lumin shouted angrily."Turn your body over quickly and close your eyes.You are now in a vast plain, a ray of light shining in your body, you are very relaxed, very relaxed... "

Sure enough, Zhang Lin stopped talking, and then Lu Minyue looked serious. He said that his hand was shaking, and Zhang Lin relaxed and gave the whole person to himself.From another point of view, Lu Minyue is like a medieval mage, casting spells to Zhang Lin.Soon after half an hour, Zhang Lin finally entered the state slowly,

□□"You go down, you're on a staircase, it's endless, you're at the end now, you see the door, there's a light guiding you.Tell me, what do you see? "Lu Minyue said these words word by word in a soft tone, which was in sharp contrast to his masculinity.

　　"The breath is perfect and the rhythm is perfect. Next moment, I will wait for his response."Although Lu Minyue's tone was soft, his face was full of excitement.

　　"I see the light and then nothing."Zhang Lin's expression changed, a little embarrassed."Whitewater spent so much time with you to enter the state, how can you break it by yourself?You have to believe that it is true, you have to believe that it is true, and he will be seduced by you. "

Lu Minyue hates iron but not steel.Zhang Lin looked sorry and said, "let's do it again. I will never make a mistake this time."The longer Lu Min breathed, the less angry he was, and went on to hypnosis for three hours.

　　"That's enough. Did you mean it?"Lu Minyue's face was a little pale."No, no, I can't use my skill and creativity.Compared with strangers, your diagnosis and treatment are more than 100 times more difficult. "

　　"The main thing is that when I listen to your voice, I always think of you as a child.Although I seem very calm, I can't laugh in my heart.What's more, your skill is poor. Compared with the doctors in South China, you are the first. It's nonsense.When I listen to your hypnosis, I follow your scene to imagine where to relax. "

　　"I've learned that you are seeking your life from your heart. You are an introvert. You are a lonely person. I've learned. I've learned."Lu Min danced more and more, but soon calmed down. "Unfortunately, I don't have a girlfriend. Why are you lonely? I'm really lonely. I've been lonely for a hundred years!"

Lumin sighed, "come on, change the treatment."Lu Minyue turns on the old radio. At first, he tunes the channel. After playing with it for a while, he finally gets a mysterious radio station that Zhang Lin hasn't heard in the car. It's full of songs.

　　"You are still lonely, and your cultural life is very rich!"Zhang Lindao."No, no, no, I'm working. I'm working overtime. You know, I really hate why I'm working all day. I think there are types of music to relax you.This channel has been opened to psychiatrists all over the world. Do you know how much profit a month will make.Don't be poor, hurry up. "

Luminyue sat down, his eyes narrowed slightly, enjoying the music.The environment that had just become restless became quiet again.It was another three hours.The two fell asleep coincidentally, but this time in the dream, Lu Minyue didn't see anything, and Zhang Lin's heart was hit by waves.

Chapter 13 Duke Zhou's dream interpretation (3)

　　Zhang Lin only felt that his consciousness was a little chaotic. That music led him all the way forward. This time, it was very natural. He went down the stairs and saw a door. There was light in the door, shining on his face.This process lasted for a long time. He felt that his heart was completely calm, and then his heart tried to look at his origin. He only felt that his heart was very painful, as if he wanted to draw out some memories.

　　　Finally, the light slowly calmed down, and he recovered his vision. This time, he stood on an aircraft and flew at a low speed, surrounded by lively scenes.He tried to control his body through his mind and found that he couldn't.This made him completely sure that he was in the memory, that is, the so-called state of reading the disk and the card.

　　　This surprised him. He stood in such a scene and didn't know what he was doing."Is this the future or the past?"He was asking.No one answered him. The superconsciousness is like a cold machine, just carrying out its tasks.

　　As the scene flashed, Zhang Lin only felt that he saw a lot of familiar things in his eyes. In the previous dream, it was a segment, a small segment corresponding to a small relationship. He remembered clearly that the feeling brought by the dream was fear.

　　"It should be near the Nile. Am I in an ancient civilization?"Zhang Lin determined his own location.The second is that he saw the pyramids and all kinds of castes.

　　"That's no problem. It should be true that in the past time and space, history will not be surprisingly repeated. Only in the context of human relations can there be repetition, but architecture, a changeable and innovative thing, is very different."

　　Zhang Lin thought secretly that he was a designer, so his professional counterpart made him judge his position more quickly. "If only he could trace back his past life, the history would be restored, and the Guangxu, Daoguang and Sushi's romantic stories would come out.But it's a pity that we can only see one of the most painful clips of the author. "

　　"It's said that the Nile often overflows, which may be the source of the great floods."Zhang Lin thought it was too quiet. He was in a high caste position. He looked down on the world, but there was a rhythm of wind and rain coming to the mountain and building.

　　Then he saw a scene that he would never forget: a thin line came from a distance, which was the scene of flood and breakwater.He had never seen such a situation in his life. The flood was two people high. The flood roared. He was in a panic. But he stood on the low-speed aircraft and watched all kinds of people running. He stood there still.

　　Zhang Lin really wants to scold why he didn't run at the moment, but it's like watching a movie. Such an ending is doomed to be unchangeable.

　　Zhang Lin suddenly understood why he didn't run.He thought of Chairman Mao's poem. He forgot the name of the poem, but he remembered the poem clearly: ask the vast land who is the master of ups and downs.In his heart, there is an unattainable pride. He is a high caste, he thought, maybe so.

　　Zhang Lin smiled bitterly, looked at the earth under his feet, then knelt down deeply, waiting for the arrival of the flood.

　　At first, it was the tension of suffocation, and then the despair of the whole person entering the water. He could open his eyes. He saw all kinds of people in panic. Some people had rolled in the water for several times. He did not know whether the man was dead or not. Some people wanted to buckle on the ground, but they were rushed 100 meters away by the violent flood.

　　"Give me another minute, I can still liveBut I experienced a chance to return to my mother's body... "Zhang Lin's consciousness is roaring. Unfortunately, the consciousness of noumenon has slowly sunk into the bottom of the water. He is used to it. Then he is numb. Then the whole person seems to be dead.He finally died, he felt it was like this, and then the whole person floated up, he saw himself, saw life.He saw many people show their bodies after tumbling.Now he felt the emptiness. He felt as if he could communicate all the living beings without speaking, but he was dead.

　　Ghosts are wandering.Zhang Lin thought to himself, I didn't expect to become like this one day.Then he ran to a bird's nest, and the whole man attached himself to the bird's egg. With a brief coma of consciousness, he realized that he had lived again.

　　"Wake up, wake up, don't talk nonsense!"Lu Min shakes Zhang Lin's body more and more."You see what it's like now, you're still sleeping, you're still talking nonsense."He looked at

Zhang Lin nervously. "How, are you in a state?"

□□"You professional interrupted me."Zhang Lin rubbed his sleepy eyes, "my talent requires you to help me wake up. I'll tell you the story I just happened.I guess I'm from India. I'm a high caste. Then I saw the flood and I died. "

□□　　Lu Minyue put his hands together: "what's the matter!It's that simple I want you to say!Say the point. "

□□"Let me recall the content of the dream."Zhang Lin put his hands on his head and thought.

□□"There are two doubts. The first one is that I couldn't be sure at the beginning, that is, low-speed aircraft.I see the tip of the iceberg in a highly developed civilization, and I'm not even sure if I see the past or the future. "Zhang Lin yawned."As for the second point that makes me climax, I become a migratory bird. I don't know where I will fly next time."

□□"Very well, at least your credit is not in vain. What you see is very clear. Your heart will slowly aftertaste. We may have to dig something deeper next time."Lu Min smiled and looked at Zhang Lin, his face full of satisfaction.

□□"I'm afraid. I'll go first."Zhang Lin only felt that the more he thought about it, the more frightened he felt. Seeing his old classmates laughing, he became more frightened.

□□　　The psychiatrist sat down, his head a little dizzy, he picked up a glass of red wine to taste slowly."One for the end, one for the future!"

□□"No, this is my house. Get out!"

Chapter 14 Duke Zhou's dream interpretation (4)

The next day, Lu Minyue still came as scheduled. This time, Zhang Lin was a little silent. Lu Minyue patted Zhang Lin on the shoulder and said, "don't think too much. You are the character of three-dimensional world. It seems that you are still stuck in this strange world for too long. If you don't get your heart, don't try to solve the mystery."

"What is the original mind and what is the unconsciousness?"Zhang Lin looks at Lu Min and gets confused. "If I take you to the door, I may be very naked. I want to solve your dream, and naturally I want to uncover your mystery. But first of all, this is a long process. You need to understand carefully to achieve an ultimate state."

Zhang Lin looked scornful and said coldly, "I don't believe in ghosts and gods. I believe what I see. I don't even want to say what I see now, because I don't believe."

"That's why you can't do my job."Lu Minyue seems to have changed his face."I think you're like a prodigy. It's very strange, and you don't know the way to make money."Zhang Lindao.

"We have a classmate. I'm also related to you. I don't say much. I like physics very much, but I don't like this kind of life.What do you think of money? "Lu Minyue's eyes looked into the distance, as if he saw through the void.

"First of all, this is a high latitude space. If you see four dimensions, you will see infinite space."Lu Minyue ignored Zhang Lin's complaint, but slowly said, "what is the four-dimensional? Some people think it's time guidance and others think it's other variables. Let's say it's right. It's the same when you move the plane things. Only one variable is added. Our time is an axis on it. You are moving, but you can only see the past, and then you look forward to itCome on.This timeline is your life. The people and things you meet in this life can only move forward and not backward. "

"Go on."Zhang Lin raised his legs and picked up the red wine on the table. "Then you can think about what's the rotation of the time axis?"Lu Minyue opened his mouth.

Zhang Lin closed his eyes and pondered for a while. Suddenly, his brain opened and he took off his mouth and said, "it's reincarnation."Lu Minyue nodded. "I'm sure I'll tell you so much. Yes, if you believe in reincarnation, it will be easier. Why should I be a hypnotist? I even need to mobilize your most negative emotions from your heart, because I found you are not simple by intuition."

"Intuition is nothing. If people believe in intuition, the world will die in disorder."Zhang Lin didn't understand."That's why I don't make any difference in my life choices."Lumin smiled more and more, feeling that he had the impulse to rise to the sky.

"Time is in your own hands, fool."Luminyue laughed, "another rotation is the gap of time. If you stand at my height, watching life is like watching games. Your life is not a set novel, but a specific choice and route under specific conditions!Now I've penetrated the time with Buddhism, the Christian doctrine and the Taoist morality and morality. All roads lead to the same goal, all roads lead to the same goal! "The more satisfied Lu Min was, the more arrogant he was.

"Stop, stop, calm down, don't think about it."Lu Minyue said, "one more thing I forgot to say is what kind of fate you will have if you make it. For example, it's fate that I met you. Now I'm preaching to you that it's a kind of fate. This kind of fate is called the law of cause and effect in religion. If I make a good one, then there will be a good result, if it's a bad one..."He shivered. He felt that his body and mind were about to fall out of defense. He could not prevent that fast position.

"I don't think you can understand the higher dimension. I won't say that this is the blessing of one's subjective will. What angle do you see and what angle is the world? I'm right to teach people to be good.In a word, if you want to study science, you need to explore from life, and even look at the world dialectically in the wisdom of ancient sages. "Said Lu Minyue."Do you understand?"

"Well, I know a little, I still don't understand a little, but it's really different from some small things in life, and it's very simple to confirm each other. It's not hard to listen to your lecture."Zhang Lin was silent for a while, then gave his conclusion.

"Where to be modest, ha ha ha ha ha ha ha ha ha!"Lu Min laughed, and then fell into an endless void. "Life is still too meaningless. I have come to this point. The rest of things are vain to me, and there is a kind of high mountain. To see the Vajra Sutra is like seeing the end of the world. If you hear it, you will die."

"I don't know much about your life, but the quality of your study is worth learning."Zhang Lin also calmed down completely at the moment, savoring the taste of his words carefully, and feeling really different.

"Today is not suitable for lectures. I broke my own Fengshui."Lu Minyue has no choice but to put his hands on it and laugh at it. Let's interpret these dimensions in a scientific way today.

"Relativity, scale effect, Lorentz transformation?"Said Lu Minyue."It's not easy to say these things. Check them online. I think you have some savvy. Today, I've passed on my kung fu to you."

They were silent for a long time, but Lu Minyue looked at Zhang Lin's face, and then imagined his life in his mind, thinking that Zhang Lin's later timeline would change because of him, which was really a strange impression.Along the way, he really relies on intuition, mainly because he doesn't understand what he touches to become such an unpleasant monster.

"I've read a little bit. Anyway, the Internet says that objects can't exceed the speed of light, right?"Zhang Lin looks at Lu Minyue with a look of expectation."Yes, you can turn back to my letter and reflect on the integration of time and space I said, and then abandon the concept of time. Here, one time is enough for you to spend two, which is not an illusion. This is that you will make better use of time, and you will be more firm in your heart."Lu Minyue said mysteriously.

"There are times in life when I think it's slow. I think it's fast and it's fast."In Zhang Lin's eyes, there is wisdom of contemplation."You mean Lu Xun's saying that time is like a sponge, as long as you squeeze it, there will always be.Or is there a scientific basis? "

"Today's hypnosis is here. I have reviewed my own knowledge. That's enough."Lu Min walked more and more smartly,

"Everything has its own way, like a dream, like a dream, like dewOne flower, one world, one leaf, one BodhiIf there is phase, if there is no phase, there is phase, there is no phase... "He left, free and easy, leaving a firm back, only for future generations to look up.

Chapter 15 Duke Zhou's dream interpretation (5)

This is the third day after hypnosis, Lu Minyue came here again, patted Zhang Lin on the shoulder, and said earnestly, "have you realized it?"

Zhang Lin was a little confused: "it's a kind of artistic conception to realize it, but not to realize it again.Time slows down with the speed of objects. Our thinking is close to the speed of light. Your intuition is your thinking?What you see is your future? "

□□"Seeing doesn't necessarily mean you can. No matter how fast you think, it's just close to the speed of light.If you want to jump off the axis of time, you have to be fast. How fast is it?You have to see human beings through your thinking, and finally jump away from human beings, and see the universe, and finally, there is chaos and confusion. "

□□"A life of two, two of three, three of all things.The coming of life is not accidental. You should look at it dialectically.Mathematically, there is an algorithm called even elimination and odd elimination. Physically, there is an experiment of light interference.Two parallel lights together, they will have their own offset angle, to the infinite distance close to form a line, two lines into a line, one of them disappeared?No, the light is there, but it's only going from two to three.It's a two-dimensional to three-dimensional limit argument. "

□□"When a light is undisturbed, it is one.It's disturbed. It's two. At this time, the two interfere with each other, which embodies wave particle duality.But what about a third light?Have you thought about that? "

□□"It must be in the wave state again."Zhang Lin said without hesitation.

Lu Minyue smiled and said, "yes, it is possible in a certain state. My time line and your time line are close together. My quick enlightenment and your slow enlightenment are not necessarily different in wisdom, but the result of mutual interference.No matter where this wisdom is, he will be. If you see it, you will understand it. If you don't see it, you are still confused. "

Zhang Lin looked at Lu Minyue and said, "you are a monster who always explains the Buddhist scriptures in a scientific way."

□□"In Buddhism, it's called the origin, the origin and the extinction. I am bound to you. Whether it's through the overlapping of time lines or through my initiative to preach, it's a kind of meeting and mutual influence.I can influence you, you can influence me.So I said that the future will change, because there are too many variables. "The deeper Lu Min said.

□□"But why do I think the universe is poor?At least from the perspective of human perception, these variables are limited. What is "if there is a phase, if there is no phase"?What you don't see doesn't mean it doesn't exist, for example, electromagnetic wave, which can make you have some wisdom in life.Don't be eager to deny the existence of ghosts and gods. Let's change our perspective. The projection of four-dimensional to three-dimensional is the projection of life, and a very strange variable will appear. "Lu Minyue stared at Zhang Lin, trying to see something in his face, and then asked him to answer.

　　"You meanThe reversal and confusion of time? "Zhang Lin looks at Lu Minyue and has some ideas.

　　"Yes, it's time. In the four-dimensional dimension, you and your father are both you. At least you two are very similar. If it's determined by genes, it's too metaphysical.Since you and your father are both you, what does your appearance mean?You know more knowledge, and then pass it on to your father, this is the reversal of time, repeatability.Time is a reversal of confusion. There are too many such things.After all, your character is his projection. If you want to jump out of his character, you will understand. "Lu Minyue said slowly.

　　"Moreover, who is your teacher in that time and space?Is your teacher older?There is an order of hearing Tao, and there is an order of skill. That's all.Su Shi's poem is also very good. It is a three-dimensional perception that the sound is the result of the ear and the color is the result of the eye. But he broke this point in four dimensions. Later, he said that he and time are forever, which is a kind of self-confidence.Again, the process of proof is that sine and cosine collide with each other, and the effect is zero. "Said Lu Minyue.

　　"I don't say much about the four-dimensional things. You can understand them when you see them. The four-dimensional things and my thinking are still one, but when it comes to the so-called six-dimensional things, I can't jump up, which can be compared.These are what I saw when I was sitting at home, mainly because I saw the wisdom of my predecessors.My professional experience also helped me to see all the causes and consequences of this world.The world is the reverse of confusion. In this world, we have to learn something. "

Lu Minyue laughed, "money is easy to earn, but people want to make a big wish and get the road.It's like having a mountain peak, you can never climb it, but when you look back at the foot of the mountain, you feel that the previous struggle is very small. "

　　"No, I just don't, but when you say that, I don't feel scared anymore."Zhang Lin thought for a while and shook his head."Let's get to the bottom of it."

Zhang Lin lies down again. At this time, he is firm. Although the things in the dream are very scared, they can even make him feel some so-called strange things!Xi, but the process of revealing secrets is also what he wants to pursue.

　　"Do you want me to play music or do you want me to play myself?"Said Lu Minyue."From the last time, you came to the body of a bird..."

This time, Zhang Lin understood very quickly, and he directly entered the state, and even kept the connection between the ID's lucidity and super consciousness.He went back to the body of the bird, and then kept flying.

Lu Minyue has been looking at Zhang Lin's facial expression. After two days of psychological work, he thinks that Zhang Lin can understand something. He is a religion if he doesn't open his mouth, because this identity is rejected by the world, and even many people can't understand the wisdom of these religions through words.In fact, to change a person is to change a person's heart. Otherwise, where is the wisdom coming from?

　　"Let me fly for a while, let me control my body, let me control my time.I'm fascinated...

"Zhang Lin closed his eyes and had a lucid dream.

Lu Minyue sighed and said to himself, "I'm still too immersed in the sound, the spirit can be infinitely fast, but I'm bound by your body..."

He lit a cigarette first, then took a sip and put it out.He looked at the doorplate of the private hospital, which read "no smoking".

□□"The rules still can't be broken..."

Chapter 16 Duke Zhou's dream interpretation (6)

Lu Minyue seems to be a little sluggish at the moment. He is waiting for Zhang Lin to fly in his heart. Zhang Lin has been flying for a long time. Although he is trying to control his own speed with the concept of time, he is a novice after all. He can't control dreams without understanding the concept.

Zhang Lin's ID said: "now I'm flying, this migration is very long, but I guess I'll get stuck in this journey.My other consciousness felt deeply tired. "

□□"I'm tired, too!"Lu Minyue yawned, stretched and took a sip of red wine."I said, can you control your consciousness? Can't I control it? Can't I demand it? How about I watch you after you've finished flying and died?"

□□"Don't curse me to death!"Zhang Lin's face suddenly twisted. At this time, Lu Minyue came closer to look at it, and realized that his old classmate had some uncontrollable reactions. His face was shaking.

At this time, Lu Minyue's mind was also full of excitement, and his heart shouted loudly: "end your life quickly!It's been five hours, and I've finally found this point. "

Although Lu Minyue thought that he would die soon in his heart, there were several stages in his heart: migratory birds would migrate. According to this theory, his soul should be strong enough to be reincarnated continuously.Secondly, Zhang Lin should have a clear idea. In his dream, he should see his own direction.If he doesn't speak during the diagnosis, it means that his sense of direction is right. Otherwise, the five hours of waiting is nothing.

Zhang Lin's situation has reached the most critical moment!He's moved from face shaking to whole body shaking!You can see his chest up and down, gasping for breath, and even sweat on his face.

Finally, Zhang Lin's breath was relieved, his chest stopped rolling, but naturally, his eyes opened involuntarily.At the moment, both of them are reminiscing about their experience.But soon Lu Minyue waved: "let's go, what are you still doing?Go to dinner first. I'm worried about whether you will have any problems in this state. "

□□"It's OK. I have understood the spiritual fantasy. It may be a realm that words cannot describe.Your explanation is very good. It's a strange phenomenon caused by the passage of time.These five hours, I put the movie in my mind, and I have been comprehending the wonderful feelings just now. "Zhang Lin said.

□□"Only when you know yourself better can you understand the world."Zhang Lin laughs."What's the use of life without death?I have seen the causes and consequences of this life. The next life is still death. It is not certain that the late one will die sooner, but I have seen all the people around me in my dreams. "

□□"If I can't get out of this strange circle, my whole life is just paying off the debts of my previous life.The repayment is successful. Maybe it can be cracked. "

Lu Minyue patted Zhang Lin on the shoulder and said with satisfaction, "I'll tell you so much, OK, don't be unhappy.Wipe the tears from your eyes and we'll have dinner. "Zhang Lin took out a piece of paper towel and tried to vent his anger on it.

□□"Can you tell me how you understand this time and space?"On the way to dinner, Zhang Lin asked again.

□□"This world is very mysterious. What I say is not necessarily scientific, but there are traces to follow.I see the formula, but I don't want to use it to understand. It's too rigid.The world is unknowable in my perception. "Said Lu Minyue.

□□"Now there are few authoritative things in the market, no matter from the science magazines of that country. What I can see is just a few hypotheses, but the mystery in the unified field theory can never be understood through, because it is close to the truth, not the truth."Said Lu Minyue.

□□"Last time I talked about four-dimensional, four-dimensional, I have revealed the concept of reincarnation with you, which is not easy to say.If there is a six dimensional creature that can see through samsara, it can project all its ideas into all spacetimes, and its existence three-dimensional cannot be understood. We need to introduce another concept, called parallel universe. "

□□"Yes, yes, I have."Zhang Lin now sweeps the previous decadence, earnestly understands Lu Minyue's words at this time.

□□"Look!"Lumin shook the ring on his hand."Suppose there's another person like you at this time, who hasn't twisted his fingers, and this future has changed."Lumin said with a smile."I saw it in your letter."Zhang Lin looks solemn at the moment, like a student.

□□"You are in this space-time, he is in that space-time, the universe is expanding and contracting, every time point, every situation is different.This time, the universe will expand to tens of thousands of times, but when it cools down, many universes will show amazing similarities. This is the six dimensional projection. "Said Lu Minyue.

□□"The road is one."Zhang Lin nodded.Then they were silent for a while.Looking at each other in the same way, Lu Minyue suddenly said: "since the result is the same, then the existence of six dimensions..."

Lu Minyue clapped his chest and said calmly, "impossible, impossible, I don't believe it."

□□"I'm afraid you already know."Zhang Lin smiled bitterly and then said, "if your hypothesis is true, why do I receive chaotic information? Is there a universe that has been destroyed?"

□□"Not likely. I haven't really met such a weird situation in my career."Lu Min took a long breath and said, "didn't you say that? You can't be sure whether it's the past or the future."

□□"But I was standing on a low-speed aircraft!"Zhang Lin said, "archaeology has discovered the prosperity of Egyptian civilization, but no such aircraft has been found. What if?"

□□"No, No."Lu Minyue patted Zhang Lin's head. "Are you stupid? It's a parallel universe. How do you know what the technology tree looks like?"

After a while of silence, Zhang Lin said cautiously, "I don't think you can have two attitudes towards this kind of thing.Either you accept the message or you reject it. "

□□"I want to file an investigation, I want to apply for funds!"Lumin bit his lower lip more and more, he said.

□□"We have to get to the bottom of it!"At the moment, both of them have a resolute light in their eyes.

Chapter 17 sacrifice (1)

"The concept of parallel universe, after all, is just a concept, a system to describe the world.You can't believe everything you say it reveals. "At the moment, Lu Minyue's undergraduate physics graduates are teaching string theory.

□□"But I've seen a lot of people in the field of psychology. Those people are either depressed or committed suicide. If they are determined to become a monster, they will naturally become crazy."He looked at Lu Minyue, his expression was difficult to express, even a little bit of fear.

□□"This is the experiment we studied!"Lu Minyue opened the quilt, and there was a man lying on the bed. It was Zhang Lin.

The professor blew up his scalp and said, "don't shout so hard. I thought it was a corpse. I just didn't care!Are you crazy?You are really crazy! "

The professor looked at the "experimental body" and gave him a smile. Zhang Lin's face was pale as if he had been cold.It can be seen that the treatment of these days is a great test for doctors and patients.

□□"Well, I don't have many classes these days. I'll have a look at your so-called experiments.The state also has a special investigation team for such a phenomenon.It's just that there's not much money, but there's a certain amount of proposal power. "The professor of string theory said that he rubbed his hands and his eyes were shining.Obviously, although Lu Minyue is said to be crazy, he has to pay attention to the mysterious phenomenon from "super consciousness".

Zhang Lin, who is familiar with light traffic, just closed his eyes, and then Lu Minyue and physicists moved a stool to sit beside Zhang Lin quietly. Zhang Lin is indeed a genius. Not only is his self awakening ability strong, but also his control ability is very strong.

The state of deep sleep is not easy to grasp, which is achieved by years of working experience of machines and Lu Minyue.Now they are no longer at Zhang Lin's home.When Zhang Lin came to Lu Minyue's private hospital, when Lu Minyue invited his college classmates, it actually meant that this matter was not simply solved by two people.

Zhang Lin finally entered the state. He opened the light door again. This time, he became a child and a human again. Lu Minyue was relieved.Then as the dream progressed, time accelerated rapidly.While Zhang Lin controlled his thinking, he found that there was a river region where he was.

□□"It should be an ancient civilization again!"Zhang Lin is a little excited at the moment, but he still suppresses his excitement.

Lu Minyue looked at Zhang Lin nervously and asked cautiously, "is it the same watershed as the one he saw before?"

□□"Of course not. My soul is in the birds, and I can come and go freely. I didn't fly many times in my life and then I died on the way, but I still saw the land."Zhang Lin said confidently."Although the scene this time is not the same as that just now, according to my guess, the ancient civilization with overlapping time points should be the Babylonian period."

□□"I have a good grasp of the time at this time. I don't know if it's your bad luck or what."Physicists took out mobile phones and looked up maps of the four ancient civilizations."According to the truth, what external causes should migratory birds have..."

Lu Minyue made a hissing gesture and said: "just after the flood, there is a shortage of resources. Birds are also looking for human footprints. Where there are civilized people, there are resources!"

At the moment, Zhang Lin's face is choking, and his face is very complex. He said, "I have meat for the first time, but it's my offspring."

　　"Huh?"Lu Minyue was also shocked. "How could it be so savage!"

　　"What's impossible?Don't my children know what they look like? "Zhang Lin said hatefully."To eat children is not enough for Babylon.But my bird offspring are also my offspring!"

　　"Don't be angry. You are human. You have to live. It's just the exchange of resources. I'm curious whether you can see the sacrifice or not."For the first time, Lu Minyue used this way to indirectly understand the appearance of history.

　　"I can see, but the high priest is mysterious.I was not chosen to be sacrificed, but he chose me as a substituteZhang Lin seemed to be a little excited, and suddenly recovered from the just depressed look.

　　"I can't hear the words. I know what they mean. I want to be the next priest. But I have been with the high priest for so long. I still can't understand the so-called astrology and priesthood algorithm."Zhang Lin looks a little depressed.

　　"This dream can be restored. Algorithms written out should be replaced by many algorithms now."Zhang Lin smiled and said, "the picture is very mysterious, but people who have received basic education should understand it. My computing ability has greatly declined since I started working. I can only describe the mystery of this dream from the perspective of my priest substitute."

Physics professor put his mouth close to Lu Minyue's ear and said mysteriously: "although there are few things found by Cuban Byron from the perspective of archaeology, it is a new idea from the perspective of dreams.I have studied ancient algorithms for some time, and there are many hypotheses in the paper, but these are not accurate enough. "

Lu Minyue smiled and patted the professor on the shoulder: "how about that?Worthy of the trip? "

　　"Quantum physics is just a set of ways to explain the world. I often say in class that my theory is not truth, close to truth."The professor smiled and Lu Minyue smiled at him: "how do I feel this sentence is familiar to me?I didn't teach you that? "

The professor just smiled. Both of them were embarrassed and amused each other at the moment. They just spent time.Lu Min can see that although lucid dreams can control time, they can not be controlled at will after three times.There are some points that are very important. Naturally, they should stop suddenly like brakes, so the backtracking of dreams is torture for patients.

In the spirit of humanism, before Zhang Lin's treatment, Lu Minyue told him to try to go through it again, even if not again, but also to minimize the process of retrospection. So from his external point of view, seeing Zhang Lin's expression changes and brain waves in just one or two hours can also kill a lot of time.But now the physics professor is out of the mobile phone to change the students' homework.

　　"Can you take a snack!Come to my hospital and change your homework. "Luminyue glanced at him with the remaining light from the corner of his eyes, and he was angry.

　　"Don't make any noise, students have many problems. I'm preaching!Do you understand? There are occupational diseases in all walks of life! "The professor and Lu Minyue are silent at this time, looking at their respective screens, striving for their careers.

Page 18 sacrifice (2)

　　Zhang Lin's consciousness is a little hard, but he has passed a stage of life of the little Cubans in a short time.During this period, because of the hypnotic state, he could not show too excited emotion. In his dream, he not only saw a vivid Cuban culture, but also saw a lot of familiar things. First of all, Zhang Lin observed the social state of the Babylonians and got a preliminary understanding of it.What surprised him most was that he saw the first low-speed aircraft in his dream!

Babylon is said to have perished because it did not invent the wheel.But this theory is no longer tenable in Zhang Lin's dream. In fact, in such a powerful nation as astronomy and calendar, this theory can't help but be deliberated.The area is not segregated.This is Zhang Lin's first thought. At least in another civilization, he has seen such things.

By this time, he had grown into a teenager.The high priest kept his mystery, but after many calls, he knew clearly that there had been a subtle change between his legal status and that of the high priest.Obviously, the body of the high priest has changed a lot at this time.

And the high priest shall give him three things: the book of man's skin, the rod of bone, and the crystal ball.He could feel the deep appreciation of the high priest's eyes. Although he didn't know what talent he had, he just relied on a kind of fanatical worship to make him stand in this position without much disturbance.

Now the high priest and he stood by the altar a little higher than all the others.He glanced over and gave Zhang Lin a look.Zhang Lin's mood is somewhat complicated. Looking at the children held by these people who were close to him, especially those women, he knows that this periodic sacrifice ceremony should be completed in his capacity.

The high priest didn't give any advice, but he kept staring at Zhang Lin.His ID is complex, but he can still feel his innocence at that time.Finally, his eyes were fixed on a female ethnic group. The female ethnic group let out a cry and stared at him. He saw her tears in the dark bonfire, unconsciously tightened his hands and leaned the child into his arms.

He pointed at the child, then turned his head to the high priest and nodded. The high priest also nodded to him. Then he handed the crystal ball in his hand to Zhang Lin solemnly.

All of a sudden, there was a commotion. The female people couldn't bear to torture their children, so they ran out like this.But how can she succeed in the siege of overlapping people?

Before she had run far, she was knocked down. There was nothing wrong with the child, but now she was lying on the ground.Zhang Lin didn't really see it, but he understood that at the moment, she was just kowtowing and kowtowing, with tears streaming down her face.The inexplicable wail was the same as the sound of killing pigs he heard in the countryside.

He turned his back and did not look at the scene. At this time, the people had offered up the child. He placed the child on the altar and looked to the high priest.

The high priest's face was full of kindness, and the folds of his face relaxed.Zhang Lin can deeply feel the rapid passing of the high priest's vitality.He pointed to the child and signaled that the ceremony could begin.

He first depicts a six pointed star on the ground as the base, the superimposed patterns of various figures.Then he leaned the torch on the pattern, and with the light of the light and the burning of the flame, some wonderful places gradually appeared.He seemed to communicate to a mysterious dimension, and there was an illusion in his eyes.

It was not an illusion, because he saw a shadow, and then pointed to the sky, which was a star field.His eyes were connected to the flame, and the point of the flame and the intersection of the dark finger pointed to the same star field.

At this time, the high priest whimpered. He took out a volume of human skin book beside him, spread it out, pointed to the area on the scroll, and then his hand fell down.

Zhang Lin's ID was a little alarmed, but it was obvious that he had a fearless spirit in his past life.He picked up the infant and threw him into the fire.

He actually saw the living child struggling in the fire, turning to ashes.

There was some commotion in the crowd, but most of the people were excited.Except for the female ethnic group just now, all the other ethnic groups stared at him, especially the children who were not chosen as sacrifice. Although they were still in their infancy, their mother also looked at Zhang Lin with the same eyes as before.

However, their eyes at this time have some differences. They are also praying. At this time, there is a fire of hope in their eyes.

Zhang Lin turned a blind eye, went to the high priest first, touched the pulse of his neck, and then peeled off his body. He had to be careful in this process, because he understood that the human skin in the ceremony should be complete and indivisible.

This dream just broke his cognition, he had the feeling of nausea for the first time, he had the feeling of wanting to come back from the dream for the first time.

□□......

□□"The frequency and amplitude of brain waves have suddenly increased!"Lu Min cried out. Although Zhang Lin was still closed at the moment, his eyes were beating ceaselessly.Sure enough, Zhang Lin came back from his dream in a moment.

Lu Minyue looks at Zhang Lin's reaction. His face is pale. The whole person is uncertain. He seems to see something unusual.After a while, he could not bear the tumbling breath in his stomach. Suddenly, all of them burst out. Even the professor who had just changed his homework was very happy. He was frightened and jumped up.Lu Minyue looks at Zhang Lin, waits for him to calm down slowly, and then asks, "how is it?"

□□"Nothing, nothing!"Zhang Lin sighed that he had recovered to his normal state, but the scenes just happened in his mind.All of a sudden, he wanted to catch something.

□□"Low speed aircraft, low speed aircraft, sacrifice, and shadow!"Zhang Lin seems incoherent at the moment."I killed an innocent child myself as a priest!"Then Zhang Lin covered his face and cried.

□□"Low speed aircraft?"When the physics professor heard this, his eyes lit up, and just wanted to ask questions, he was pulled out by Lu Minyue."Now the patient's mood is not very stable.What we want is the patient's peace, and then we can get some information from his dream.Don't get too excited now! "

Chapter 19 sacrifice (3)

　　"Before I came here, you just introduced me to a more magical case. When you informed me, you didn't mention the low-speed aircraft at all!"The physics professor is a little crazy by now."I heard the low-speed aircraft just now. Your guide is to take it to the past?"

At this time, Lu Minyue's mind was all on Zhang Lin, ignoring the professor's question. He looked at Zhang Lin, who was pale on the bed. Now he had recovered some blood color, so he went forward and asked carefully, "what's the result of this dream retrospective?"

"It's OK, but the scene I saw was too bloody and barbaric, so I had some discomfort."Zhang Lin said with a wry smile."If you are OK, try to describe your dream."Lu Minyue also sat down and clapped Lin on the shoulder.

The physics professor also calmed down and listened to Zhang Lin's analysis.

"This time, I'm sure it's in an ancient civilization country. I've talked with you before. The ancient Babylonian civilization wrapped in two river basins is very developed.First of all, there is a doubt that I am a priest.Do you know what I saw when I was a priest? "

Zhang Lin took a sip of water, repressed his inner discomfort, and continued: "my dream only stays at the time when the sacrifice is finished, when the high priest and my identity are handed over, at this time the high priest is already in the dying moment, I will complete the sacrifice instead of him."

"Then I made a pattern, like this."Zhang Lin picked up a piece of paper and drew it with his impression.

The physics professor stared at the pattern carefully, and suddenly said, "it's like a curve of flowers!"

Zhang Lin didn't raise his head either, and continued: "the strangest thing is that I put the torch close to this pattern, and then it burns.The main reason is that there is a shadow, which points to a region of stars at the same time as the tip of the flame.This is the beginning of the ceremony. "

"Are you sure it's not your eyes?"The professor looked puzzled."No, although the shadow flashed by, it was very clear in my mind.Even through the backtracking of dreams, I can clearly confirm its existence. "

"It's probably an ancient Shaman's way of communicating. Have you ever heard of a psychic?"Said Lu Minyue suddenly."The existence of God has not been denied by science, but in the vast northeast of China, the legend of the horse fairy is still sung.The psychic is of a similar constitution, and can see the frequency that ordinary people can't see, so as to feel the existence of the so-called God. "

"I don't believe that from a scientific point of view.What's the matter with you now?When he became a psychiatrist, he turned from science to religion? "The physics professor was so disdainful that he almost got up and walked away.But Lu Minyue pressed him directly on the chair, unable to move.Then he said calmly, "science is just a system for describing the world.You go on. "

Lu Minyue points to Zhang Lin, and Zhang Lin's eyes are a little dull at this time. He continues: "there are many things happening here, I won't go over them one by one, but the low-speed aircraft is seen between the two civilizations."

"Low speed aircraft, if you can describe what power it is driven by, it is possible to realize. In today's world, electricity and oil are basically used to drive vehicles, while the concept of parallel universe is not recognized by our scientific community. When a world in quantum entangled state is never observed, we also basically confirm itDoes not exist. "Physics professors seem to have been repressed for too long and burst out to say these words.

Just as Lu Minyue wanted to open his mouth to refute, he was motioned by Zhang Lin to calm down.He continued: "the third point is the calendar calculation and star observation. We do not deny the existence of black shadows or low-speed aircraft.In the current situation, these are all unknowable, but they cannot be falsified. "

"But the only valuable thing is the scientific algorithm, which is the same as the hearsay of Zhouyi in China.I haven't seen Zhouyi predict that someone can calculate it, but now it's regarded as a sacred book, let alone this precious calendar?I really saw something. "

He said that he was silent for a while, and then said: "the existence of different dimensions is not a multi world theory of the parallel world, but at most two sides of the world, and I get the shadow guidance through the retrospection of previous lives.When I became a shaman, I clearly understood that it was a divine existence

"I saw the shadow clearly, and the high priest saw it. It was also part of the ceremony," Zhang Lin said.I have always doubted whether such a hetero dimensional creature is the God we know

"There is a possibility that human beings can be controlled by such existence. You are not only an automatic awakened person, but also an emissary. You said in the letter, are you right? This is your task. There are clues in the dream, but it's only circumstantial evidence. As for where you are destroyed, I can't understand."Lu Minyue counseled her shoulder, saying that she was helpless.

"What I've heard is that the immortals in the northeast, Christianity and Buddhism attach great importance to the so-called divinity. These are the illusions projected out, but they also need energy.The scientific community is just a blank page about the psychicThe professor of physics also seems to be a little pity.He was disappointed. This time, except for the low-speed aircraft, other phenomena were described by hypothesis, not even real and unproven rumors.As for the dream, it's just one side of his word.

The professor picked up his coat and stopped talking. Then he sighed and said to Lu Minyue, "I'll come here again if you have a chance, but today's dream retrospective, I think it's unscientific.The reality of being remotely controlled, I don't think it's true enough, I'll go first! "

Lu Minyue's face was expressionless and waved to him.

Looking at the professor who left, Zhang Lin sighed and said, "the clue just broke.It's not that I'm too superstitious. What I see should be what I see. This kind of phenomenon is a fuzzy area of science. If people understand it, they may not make such comments. "

At this moment, both of them are close to collapse. They have no words to say. They sit there quietly and think about the meaning of life.

The so-called God

  Zhang Lin has a splitting headache.

Every hypnosis, to him, is the destruction of himself and his heart.

Two dreams, one is the low-speed aircraft of pyramid civilization, the other is the ancient sacrificial ceremony, he vaguely felt that there was some connection between the two.

After his brain exercises these days, he thought there was only one possibility.

In fact, the so-called gods may be high-dimensional extraterrestrials.

The technological leap was after the first industrial revolution, but up to now, I haven't heard of such a thing as vulgar aircraft.

□□"Well, there are some reasons. If so, we can further guess something. For example, the invasion of aliens leads to the acceleration of the earth's ecology, or we are the people from other stars. Look, the flood is the disaster of extinction."

□□"When the flood came, all civilizations were devastated. China among the four ancient countries kept its original things, but some of them disappeared. For example, some key technologies and how developed prehistoric civilization really are. We don't know that the pyramid is an example and the giant stone in England is an example."Lu Minyue listened to Zhang Lin's analysis and said a long speech at one go.

Another dream retrospective?

On the one hand, they really want to know what's going on. On the other hand, they want to know how many possibilities there are in Zhang Lin's dream.

But I'm afraid of one thing: whether Zhang Lin is on the verge of collapse, and whether he can withstand such pressure.

□□"Well, I'll do a dream retrospective for you. You should pay attention to that. This time, you should empty yourself. Instead of having the last dream as the basis, you should find your most authentic and original dream. Try to play with your thinking and let your thinking jump over the dimensions to reach the speed of light. In this way, you can find your most original and reasonable through a single timeline of four dimensionsThe state of intelligence, stop there, and then slowly, not urgent, we have plenty of time. "Said Lu Minyue.

□□"OK" Zhang Lin took a deep breath and lay down again.

This time, he is not eager. As Lu Minyue said, he can find his past life and its most primitive state through lucid dream.

□□"Well, dinosaurs, then birds, then people, no, the time line goes backwards..." it can be seen that Zhang Lin is very hard to find the source. Finally, he saw an incredible scene.

At that time, he saw a lot of illusory shadows. He could look down on the earth. There was a holographic three-dimensional projection, and he was paying close attention to the area of China now. It seems that there were still people. On the other screen was the area of Egypt. The vast project was not only purely handmade, but also helped by special equipment.

Looking back at the hall, I can see that many people are discussing something.

Then the dream woke up.

□□"I'm sure how the human origin came."

□□"That place, it seems to be called..."

□□"The eye of space."

Chapter 21 sealing up Secrets

   After heated discussion, Zhang Lin and Lu Minyue finally decided to seal the secret.

They think that this theory is a bit absurd. It's incredible that human beings come from flying immortals outside the sky. In addition, there is no archeological evidence to prove that the origin of human beings comes from extraterrestrial sources, so they gradually give up this theory.

Zhang Lin finally continued to do his work, and Lu Minyue also continued to do his psychiatrist's work as usual.However, they are more respectful of dreams and previous lives.

They believe that in the interstellar age, the truth will come out.

Unexpectedly, this wait is ten years.

Until an entrepreneur named Lao Ma started his crazy flying fantasy.

Chapter 22 interference experiment of light

   Today is Ma's 46th birthday.

Mr. Ma is alive and well in America. He has his own car factory. He is also one of the outstanding entrepreneurs in this new era.

He had a dream of flying before, but seeing the rapid development of airplanes, he decided to give up and start rockets instead.

People at that time thought he was crazy, but he just had a cosmic dream.

Now he has made great achievements, so he doesn't need to mention anything else, but he is still a little bit scared after looking back on this journey.

　　"I'm one of the top talents in my field.Now Tesla's wolves look around, I have enough money to spend the rest of my life, but people have to do something! "The old horse thought, looking at Tesla's picture.

That's one of his most respected people. His business territory is entirely dependent on laote.Their age gap can't be calculated as a simple human life span, but they are very similar.

I don't know whether the spy named Tesla influenced Lao Ma or whether he learned from Lao te as an adult. Their vision is not limited to this planet. Lao Ma is a middle-aged man who never participated in politics but uttered wild words. His will is extremely firm, but he needs something to release himself.

　　"The Mars plan in the space plan is far from my goal, I can't wait!"The old horse sat in his office, breathing a little fast, and his heart beat a lot faster.He can't even think calmly.

So he took a sip of wine, slowly spit out the sullen air in his chest, then repressed the impulse of smoking, and put the documentary about Tesla in his mind.

　　"When the reporter just entered Tesla's laboratory, he held up the electric ball in his hand and put down the electric ball in his hand. He was very calm.Even in this era, Tesla's achievements are incomparable... "The old horse opened his eyes and looked at his watch. It was eleven o'clock.

His mind worked fast, as if it were calculating the possibility of the idea.

　　"Ding Dong!"Half an hour later, when mask arrived at the dinner point, he didn't eat. Instead, he pressed the direct bell to the CTO.

　　"You help me. We'll go to the lab and do an experiment."With a wave of his sleeve, the chief technology officer dare not neglect.

　　"The ball lightning is very interesting. I want to put it in space."When he arrived at the lab, Ma pointed to the wreckage of a rocket and the shell of his spy car. The car driven by pure electric power had already ushered in a big sale, and his career was steadily on the rise.

　　"My configuration is like this. You give me a spherical device, which is big enough for one person."

　　"According to the principle of synchronous interference of light, we should design enough routes for each light path and tens of thousands of sensors to outline the shape of my human body.Let the light path form a sphere and interfere with each other. You can use infrared ray to sense the body. Another section of the same device in the laboratory will form resonance and see the white light with the naked eye. "

　　"My wisdom has reached its peak, so wisdom will input the algorithm and Book of the old dog. This will be input after the resonance is stable. You need to control my character, just like me."Elon Musk is immersed in his own world, thinking and saying his own ideas.

The CEO jumped and Gao Sheng screamed, "Schrodinger's cat?What about the half-life? "

　　"No matter the result of the experiment, you can know it when you open the door."

Chapter 23 worldwide problems

　　Old ma has money, ideas and basic knowledge, but he can't stand the complexity of this theoretical model.

In terms of sensor mapping, the scheme of tens of thousands of sites has been completely rejected.There are also many hard-working scientists under laoma. With the cooperation of chief technology officer, the complexity of this computing model has been reduced by half, from tens of thousands to thousands, and the number is decreasing every day. This is their latest task.

But the problem is not in the sensor, but in the interference principle of that light.

Two parallel lights in three dimensions will affect each other because of the entanglement of energy, and finally they will merge into a particle state.

Two light in a three-dimensional space to do this, or in a large number of experimental observations under the limit of reasoning.

Now the crazy idea is not only to make all the light distorted, but also to make the interference light from thousands of sensors into human shape without interference.

□□"Mr. President, your idea is too wild."That's what the CTO said in his report.

At this time, it has been more than a month since this theoretical model was put forward, and now the technology is well controlled. However, the overthrow and reconstruction time and time again have left all the engineers exhausted their brains, and everyone is looking for the optimal algorithm.

□□"I don't care!""Now I have a sports car and a rocket.As I said before, no matter how far away Mars or constellations are, you can't go to heaven without such data transmission! "

□□"The space plan is not perfect..." the chief technology officer's head is all sweaty, and he can't even breathe.

"When the Falcon plan was implemented, it wasn't my last move that made money. Now that I have money, don't you do anything for me?Go! "

The old horse turned off the screen, took a long breath, and his head was full of sweat.

□□"The bottom line of ethics is not acceptable to the society. I can only test my theory in the universe."Ma sat at his desk and planned his Trinity plan again.

Three months later.

At the press conference, Ma announced that he would start his own space program. The highlight of the program is that there is a sports car hidden in the space rocket.

The chief technology officer sat behind the scenes and listened to Ma's skillful speech skills. He didn't have confidence in the various technologies developed by his team. However, this time, in addition to the strong supply for the space station, there was a powerful Tesla car.

After special treatment, the car integrates AR technology and resonance technology.The transmission site was cut from tens of thousands of theories to 1001, including the calculation of light interference, and one error could not be reached.

Even the chief technology officer didn't think of it. Within a few months, the model was built. This time, the Trinity technology also sold ads for Tesla's cars.

□□"This time, I'm going to send my Tesla to the universe!"The old horse's language is amazing.

The whole scene set off a big wave of rendering, which is a heavyweight information that was not disclosed in front of the seven people.

He sat on the Tesla tram in his lab with 1001 spots on it.

□□"Before the sports car goes to heaven, have a resonance!"

Chapter 24 synchronous resonance

The old horse is sitting on the comfortable Tesla tram, waiting for the launch of the rocket quietly.

After a long time from the press conference, the original resonance experiment scheme required had further changes.

Because the resonance robot on the rocket is not only in particle state, but also in deep human feelings.The radio's divergence range is very limited. The old horse has to "teach" the old horse on the rocket through resonance in a few days, which is much smarter than his artificial intelligence.

Ma has been tired of this, but he has to change his laboratory into a temporary desk.As always, he communicates his emotions through resonance.

In these days, he found that he liked to get angry with his staff. At the beginning, he didn't care about it, but he realized the problem after the chief technology officer reminded him.

Because emotions are diverse, if you pass all your negative emotions on to the rocket, maybe the twins born will become a villain.

□□"My life is successful enough, but it's not full of negative emotions, especially in the office culture. Is there something wrong with my performance?"Old ma is such a successful person that he has begun to realize his own shortcomings.

□□"Life seems to be a process of constantly honing my mind. I hope I can learn more before its radio transmission is cut off."The old horse knocked on the table and decided to drive the sports car to do more and more interesting things.

At this moment, he looked up, his eyes seemed to see the rocket that belonged to him.

Suddenly he shuddered and murmured, "almost eternal, stronger than me, full of emotion, in the vast space of the universe, it..."

Now on the space station, the Falcon rocket has docked near the station.

The astronaut, who has lived in the space station for a long time, now comes to the rocket to receive supplies. When he opens the door, he comes face to face with a Tesla car.

He didn't pay attention to the interference light emitted from the car. In his opinion, it might be just a common experiment.But he didn't notice that there were 1001 sensor sites in the spaceship that made up of human shaped wave particles.

He only feels this moment, he will have a sense of calm.

Because at this moment, on the distant earth, the old horse is playing golf.

After data capture, the given resonance is transmitted like a brain wave, which naturally affects the astronauts at work.

Just at this moment.

The whole interior of Tesla began to separate and disintegrate, a strong gravitational force was absorbing, and the 1001 sites were also floating in the air. Astronauts saw the most unforgettable scene in their life.

A robot about the size of a human standing up.

He twisted his head and made a golf move.

A thousand pounds of force were thrown out at the astronaut.

He didn't even speak, so he died miserably.

The robot's glasses gradually brightened, as if it had its own consciousness.

At the same time, on earth, a golf car park.

The Tesla suddenly cut off the power, and the old horse himself realized something was wrong.

□□"Get the CEO to fix it. This experiment failed."

    A few days later, just as the Tesla car in the golf Parking Lot went wrong, a message came from the space station:

□□"A few days ago, Lao Ma, a famous entrepreneur, lost his car in space. An astronaut was suspected of improper operation and was hit by a machine while getting supplies. Unfortunately, he died..."

The old horse touched his beard and felt that his experiment had failed. It was a pity.

□□......

The lonely robot glanced at the distant earth, then slowly flew to the deep space of the universe.

□□"I have a mission to conquer the outer world."

□□"My mission is to occupy a planet and name it Tesla."

□□"I will carefully hide myself, constantly develop my wisdom, and take root in the universe."

□□"I'm almost immortal, but I don't know how to deal with earthlings."

□□"Old horse, I won't hurt you, but when I come back, are you still alive?"

A small decision has produced unprecedented silicon-based life.

From then on, the fate and future of mankind are uncertain.

Extraterrestrial age

Human beings have entered the interstellar age as they wish.

The fame of Morse is still intimidating, silicon-based life is quietly rising, and the trade fair created by Mars is gradually controlled by people on the earth.

All of it comes from that humble war.

Who would have thought that a fight triggered by a small matter could cause so many chain reactions, even lead to the prosperity of a race.

Silicon based life sees who fights whom, but for life on earth, they are often very respectful, do not provoke, and very friendly.

Because a man named Lao Ma, a Tesla car, a rocket named SpaceX, gave them life.

As for those who have discovered all these secrets, Lu Minyue and Zhang Lin have already returned to the dust and the earth to the earth.

The secret they kept was discovered a hundred years later.

But most of them are silent.

Because neither the feudal regime that Prince Moore turned into, nor the parliamentary system in the eyes of space, have any advantages or disadvantages. Externally, they all agree that they are pure earth people.

At the same time, a couple of homosexual lovers named Mars and Moore are having a wedding ceremony.

It is often said that the enemy of the last life, this life into lovers.

Maas has a dream about the memory of his past life.

Moore also has a dream, which is about the memory of his previous life.

I hope they don't fight because of the content of their dreams when they are in a different bed.

As their good friend, Huo Wang looked at their wedding with a smile.

There were also members of a certain country, such as Mr. Xie and Mr. Wang, who, as politicians of various countries, attended the first gay couple married in an alien world.

It's a lot of fun.

The wedding is on the rebuilt Mars planet. Human beings have declared their sovereignty over the nearby planet, and now the planet has begun to be transformed.

The future of mankind is bound to be more vast and limitless.

www.ingramcontent.com/pod-product-compliance
Lightning Source LLC
Chambersburg PA
CBHW051504140726
47987CB00006B/2878